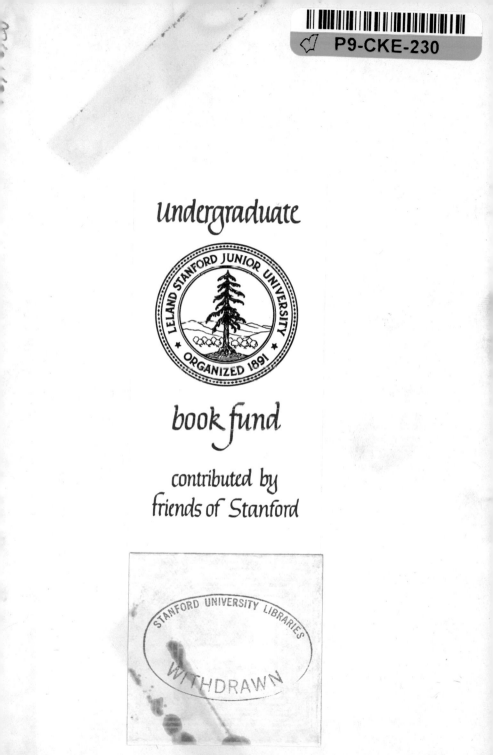

Undergraduate

book fund

contributed by
friends of Stanford

The Investigation

The Investigation

STANISŁAW LEM

Translated from the Polish by
Adele Milch

A Continuum Book
THE SEABURY PRESS
New York

The Seabury Press
815 Second Avenue
New York, N.Y. 10017

English translation copyright © 1974 by The Seabury Press, Inc.
Designed by Carol Basen
Printed in the United States of America

Original edition: *Śledztwo,* Wydawnictwo Literackie, Cracow, 1959, 1969

The Investigation

1,

Rattling rhythmically at each floor, the old-fashioned elevator moved upward past glass doors decorated with etchings of flowers. It stopped. Four men emerged and walked down the corridor toward a pair of leather-covered doors.

The doors swung open.

"This way, gentlemen," gestured someone standing just inside.

Gregory was the last one in, right behind the doctor. Compared to the brightly lit corridor, the room was almost dark. Through the window the bare branches of a tree were visible in the fog outside.

The Chief Inspector sat down behind his high, dark desk, which was enclosed by a low ornamental railing. Except for two telephones, an intercom, his pipe, his eyeglasses, and a small piece of chamois cloth, there was nothing on the polished wood surface.

Seating himself in an upholstered armchair on one side of the room, Gregory noticed Queen Victoria eying them from a small portrait on the wall behind the desk. The Chief Inspector looked at each of the men in turn as if counting them or trying to memorize their faces. One of the side walls was covered by a huge map of southern England; on the wall opposite there was a dark shelf lined with books.

"Gentlemen," the Chief Inspector said at last, "I want you to go over every aspect of this case. Since the official record has been my only source of information, I think we should start with a brief summary. Farquart, perhaps you can begin."

"Certainly, sir, but I don't know anything about the beginning of the case except what's in the reports."

"There were no reports at the very beginning," commented Gregory somewhat too loudly. Everyone turned to look at him. With exaggerated casualness he began to rummage energetically in his pocket as if looking for a cigarette.

Farquart straightened up in his chair.

"The affair began around the middle of last November, but there may have been some earlier incidents that were ignored at the time. The first report to the police was made three days before Christmas, but an investigation in January showed that these corpse incidents began much earlier. The report was made in the town of Engender, and it was, strictly speaking, semiofficial in character. Plays, the local undertaker, complained to the commander of the district police station, who happens to be his brother-in-law, that someone was moving the bodies around during the night."

"What exactly did this moving consist of?" The Chief Inspector was methodically cleaning his glasses.

"The bodies were left in one position in the evening and found in different positions the following morning. Strictly speaking, only one body was involved—apparently a certain drowned man who—"

"Apparently?" the Chief Inspector repeated in the same indifferent tone.

Farquart straightened himself even more in his chair.

"No one thought the incident was important at the time," he explained, "and when we finally began collecting evidence it was hard to get the exact details. The undertaker isn't completely sure anymore whether the body involved was actually the drowned man's. In fact the whole report is somewhat irregular. Gibson, the Engender police commander, decided not to log any of this because he thought—"

"Do we have to go over all this again?" shouted a man

4

who was sprawled in a chair next to the bookshelf. His legs were crossed so high that a line of bare skin was visible above his gold-colored socks.

"I'm sorry, but it's absolutely necessary," Farquart answered in a dull voice without looking at him. The Chief Inspector put on his glasses, and his face, until now a total blank, took on a kindly expression.

"We can do without the formal aspects of the investigation for the time being," he said. "Please go on, Farquart."

"Whatever you say, Chief Inspector. The second report was made in Planting, eight days after the first. Someone moving corpses at night in the cemetery mortuary again. The dead man was a stevedore named Thicker—he died after a long illness that almost bankrupted his family."

Farquart glanced out of the corner of his eye at Gregory, who was shifting around impatiently.

"The funeral was scheduled for the morning. When the family showed up at the mortuary they noticed that the body was lying face downward—that is, the back was facing upward—and that its hands were open, which gave them the impression that Thicker . . . had come back to life. At least that's what the family believed. Before long, rumors about some kind of trance were circulating in the neighborhood; people said that Thicker had only seemed to be dead, then woke up, found himself in a coffin, and died of fright, this time for good.

"The whole story was nonsense," Farquart continued. "A local doctor had certified Thicker's death beyond any shadow of a doubt. But as the rumors spread through the surrounding area, attention was drawn to the fact that people had been talking for some time about so-called moving corpses that changed position during the night."

"What does 'for some time' mean?" asked the Chief Inspector.

"There's no way of knowing. The rumors referred to incidents in Shaltam and Dipper. At the beginning of January the local forces made a cursory investigation, but they didn't take the matter too seriously, so they weren't very systematic. The evidence given by the local people was partly prejudiced, partly inconsistent, and as a result the investigation was worthless. In Shaltam it involved the body of one Samuel Filthey, dead of a heart attack. According to the gravedigger, who happens to be the town drunk, Filthey is supposed to have 'turned over in the coffin' on Christmas night. No one can substantiate the story. The incident in Dipper involved the body of an insane woman that was found in the morning on the floor next to the coffin. According to the neighbors, the woman's stepdaughter, who hated her, slipped into the funeral home during the night and threw her out of her coffin. The truth is, there are so many stories and rumors that it's impossible to get your bearings. It all boils down to one person giving you the name of an alleged eyewitness, and the 'witness' sending you to someone else, and so on. . . .

"The case would have been dropped as a sure *ad acta,*" Farquart began speaking faster, "but on January sixteenth the corpse of one James Trayle disappeared from the mortuary in Treakhill. Sergeant Peel, on detail from our C.I.D., investigated the incident. The corpse was removed from the mortuary sometime between midnight and five in the morning, when the undertaker discovered that it was missing. The deceased was a male . . . maybe forty-five years old—"

"You're not sure?" the Chief Inspector interrupted. He was sitting with his head bent as if peering at himself in a highly polished mirror. Farquart cleared his throat.

"I am sure, but that's the way it was told to me. . . . Anyway, the cause of death was poisoning by illuminating gas. It was an unfortunate accident."

"Autopsy?" said the Chief Inspector, raising his eyebrows. He leaned over to the side and pulled a handle which opened the casement windows. A whiff of damp air flowed into the warm, heavy atmosphere of the room.

"There was no autopsy, but we're convinced it was an accident. Six days later, on January twenty-third, there was another incident, this time in Spittoon. The missing body belonged to one John Stevens, a twenty-eight-year-old laborer in a distillery. He died the day before, after inhaling poisonous fumes while cleaning one of the vats. The body was taken to the mortuary around three in the afternoon. The caretaker saw it for the last time around nine in the evening. In the morning it wasn't there. Sergeant Peel looked into this incident also, but nothing came of this investigation either, mainly because at the time we still hadn't thought of linking these two incidents with the earlier ones . . ."

"Please keep your comments to yourself for the time being. Right now I want to concentrate on the facts," the Chief Inspector said, smiling pleasantly at Farquart. He placed his shriveled hand on the desk. Gregory couldn't help staring: the hand seemed to be completely bloodless, not a vein was visible.

"The third incident took place within the limits of Greater London in Lovering, where the Medical School has its new dissecting laboratory," Farquart continued in a dull voice, as if he had lost all interest in going on with his lengthy story. "The body of one Stewart Aloney disappeared; he was fifty years old, dead of a chronic tropical disease contracted while he was a sailor on the Bangkok run. This incident took place nine days after the other disappearances, on February second—strictly speaking, the night of the second going on the third. After this one the Yard took over. The investigation was conducted by Lieutenant Gregory, who later took command of one more case: the disappearance of a corpse from the mortuary of a suburban cemetery in Bromley on February twelfth—the incident involved the body of a woman who died after a cancer operation."

"Thank you," said the Chief Inspector. "Why isn't Sergeant Peel here?"

"He's sick, Chief Inspector, he's in the hospital," Gregory answered.

"Is that so? What's wrong with him?"

The lieutenant hesitated.

"I'm not sure, but I think it has something to do with his kidneys."

"Lieutenant, tell us about your investigation."

Gregory cleared his throat, took a deep breath, and, flicking an ash into the ashtray, spoke in an unexpectedly quiet voice.

"I don't have much to brag about. All the corpses disappeared at night, there was no evidence on the scene, no signs of forcible entry. Besides, forcible entry wouldn't have been necessary since mortuaries aren't usually locked, and those that are could probably be opened with a bent nail by a child. . . ."

"The dissecting lab was locked," said Sorensen, the medical examiner, speaking for the first time. He was sitting with his head bent backward as if to avoid drawing attention to its unpleasant angular shape, and with one finger he was massaging the swollen skin under his eyes.

It suddenly occurred to Gregory that Sorensen had done well in choosing a profession in which he associated mainly with the dead. He nodded to him with almost courtly courtesy.

"You took the words right out of my mouth, Doctor. There was an unlocked window in the room from which the corpse disappeared—in fact, it was open, as if someone had gone out through it."

"He had to get in first," Sorensen interrupted impatiently.

"A brilliant observation," Gregory replied, then regretted his words and peeked at the Chief, who remained silent, unmoving, as if he hadn't heard anything.

"The laboratory is on the first floor," the lieutenant continued after an awkward silence. "According to the janitor, the window was locked along with all the others. He swears that all the windows were locked that night—says he's absolutely certain because he checked them himself. The frost was setting in and he was afraid the radiators would freeze if the windows were open. Like most dissecting labs, they hardly give enough heat as it is. I talked to Professor Harvey—he's in charge of the place. He thinks very highly of the janitor, says he takes his work a little too seriously but that he's honest and we can believe anything he tells us."

"Are there any possible hiding places in the laboratory?" the Chief Inspector asked. He looked around at the group as if he had suddenly become aware of their presence again.

"Well, that . . . would be out of the question, Chief Inspector. No one would be able to hide without the janitor's help. There's no furniture except for the dissecting tables, no dark corners or alcoves . . . in fact, nothing at all except a few closets for the students' coats and equipment, and even a child couldn't fit into any of them."

"Do you mean that literally?"

"Sir?"

"That they're too small for a child," the Chief Inspector said quietly.

"Well . . ." The lieutenant wrinkled his brow. "A child might manage to squeeze into one, but at best only a seven- or eight-year-old."

"Did you measure the closets?"

"Yes." The answer was uttered without hesitation. "I measured all of them because I thought one might be bigger than the others. They all turned out to be the same size. Aside from the closets, there are some toilets, washrooms, and classrooms; a refrigerator and a storeroom in the basement; the professor's office and some teachers' rooms upstairs. Harvey says that the janitor checks each of the rooms every night, sometimes more than once—in my opinion, he tends to overdo it. Anyway, no one could have managed to hide there."

"What about a child?" the Chief Inspector asked in a quiet voice. He took off his eyeglasses as if to soften the sharpness of his gaze. Gregory shook his head violently.

"No, it would have been impossible. A child couldn't have opened the windows. They have locks at the top and bottom, released by levers set in the window frames. Just like here." Gregory pointed to the window, from which a cold draft was entering the room. "The levers are very tight and it's hard to move them. Even the janitor complained about it. Besides, I tried them myself."

"Did he call your attention to the fact that the levers are tight?" Sorensen asked, smiling inscrutably in a way that irritated Gregory. He would have preferred to let the question pass without an answer, but the Chief Inspector was looking at him expectantly, so he replied without much enthusiasm.

"The janitor didn't mention it until he saw me opening and closing them. He's worse than an old maid. A terrible pain in the neck," Gregory added emphatically, looking, as if by chance, at Sorensen. "He was very pleased with himself too. Of course that's natural enough for someone his age," he added in a conciliatory manner. "He's about sixty years old, sclero—" Gregory stopped abruptly, embarrassed. The Chief Inspector wasn't any younger than that. He searched desperately for a way to get around the obvious meaning of his concluding words but couldn't think of anything. The other men remained absolutely still, their silence arousing Gregory's resentment. The Chief Inspector put on his glasses.

"Are you finished?"

"Yes sir," Gregory faltered, "yes. At least as far as these three incidents are concerned. In the last case, though, I looked over the surrounding area very carefully—I was particularly interested in any unusual activity near the lab that night. The constables on duty in the neighborhood hadn't noticed anything suspicious. Also, when I took over the case I tried to find out as much as I could about the earlier incidents; I talked to Sergeant Peel and I went to all the other places but I didn't find a thing, not one piece of evidence of any kind. Nothing, absolutely nothing. The woman who died of cancer and the laborer both disappeared in similar circumstances. In the morning, when someone from the family arrived at the mortuary, the coffin was empty."

"Yes," said the Chief Inspector. "That will be all for now. Mr. Farquart, will you continue?"

"Of course, sir. Do you want to hear about the more recent cases, sir? Right, whatever you say, sir."

"He should be in the Navy," Gregory thought, sighing to himself. "He always acts like he's at the morning flag raising, and he'll never change."

"The next disappearance took place in Lewes seven days later, on February nineteenth. It involved a young stevedore who was run over by a car—ruptured liver with internal bleeding. The operation was a success, as the doctors say, but the patient didn't survive. Anyway, the body disappeared before dawn. We were able to pinpoint the time because around three o'clock that morning a certain Burton died. His sister—he lived with a sister—was so afraid to stay alone with the deceased in the same apartment that she woke up the local undertaker. The body was delivered to the funeral home at exactly three in the morning. Two employees put it next to the stevedore's body. . . ."

"You were going to say something?" asked the Chief Inspector.

11

Farquart bit his mustache.

"No . . ." he said after a moment.

The steady drone of airplane engines could be heard outside the building. Overhead, an unseen airplane flew past on its way southward. The windowpanes rattled in quiet unison.

"That is," Farquart added with an air of decision, "in arranging the newly delivered body, one of the employees moved the stevedore's body because it was in his way. Well . . . he claims it wasn't cold."

"Hmm," the Chief Inspector murmured, as if commenting on the most ordinary thing in the world. "It wasn't cold? And how did he explain it? What were his exact words?"

"He said it wasn't cold," Farquart spoke reluctantly, pausing between words. "I know it sounds idiotic . . . ridiculous, but he insists on it. He claims he mentioned it at the time, but the other employee doesn't remember a thing. Gregory questioned both of them separately, twice. . . ."

The Chief Inspector, without saying a word, turned to the lieutenant.

"Well . . . uh . . . he talks too much. Not reliable at all," Gregory explained quickly. "At least that's my impression. He's one of those clowns who will do anything to get some attention, ready to give you his version of the history of the world at the drop of a hat. He insisted it was a trance or 'something worse'—those are his words. Frankly, he surprised me. People who work professionally with corpses usually don't believe in trances—it goes against their experience."

"What do the doctors say?"

Gregory was silent, yielding the floor to Farquart. Apparently unhappy that such a minor matter was receiving so much attention, Farquart shrugged his shoulders.

"The stevedore died the day before. Signs of rigor mortis were clearly evident. . . . He was as dead as a doornail."

"Anything else?"

"Yes. Like all the other missing bodies, he was dressed for burial. The only body that wasn't dressed was Trayle's —the one that disappeared in Treakhill. The undertaker was supposed to dress him the following day because the family didn't want to give him any clothing at first. That is, they took the clothing away after the body was brought in. When they came back with different clothing the body wasn't there anymore. . . ."

"What about the other incidents?"

"The body of the woman with the cancer operation was dressed also."

"How?"

"Well . . . in a dress."

"What about shoes?" the Chief Inspector asked, his voice so soft that Gregory had to lean forward to hear him.

"Yes, shoes also."

"And the last one?"

"The last one . . . Well, it wasn't dressed, but a black cloth disappeared from the mortuary at the same time, or so it seems. The cloth was used to close off a small alcove. It was attached to a curtain rod by some small metal rings. There were still a few shreds of material on the rings."

"Was it torn?"

"No, the rod is so thin that it would have snapped if any-one had given it a good pull. The shreds—"

"Did you try to break the rod?"

"No."

"Then how do you know it would have snapped?"

"Well, by sight. . . ."

The Chief Inspector asked these questions quietly, star-ing at the reflection of the window in the glass door of a cabinet; he acted as if distracted by something else, but he shot out his questions so rapidly that Farquart could hardly keep up with him.

"Good," the Chief Inspector concluded. "Were the shreds examined?"

"Yes. Dr. Sorensen . . ."

The medical examiner stopped massaging his pointed chin. "The cloth was torn off the rod. To be exact, it had been frayed to the breaking point but it was definitely not cut. That's certain. It looked . . . as if someone had bitten it off. I conducted several tests. Under the microscope it looks the same way."

In the momentary silence that followed, a distant airplane engine was heard, its sound muffled by the fog.

"Was anything else missing besides the curtain?" the Chief Inspector asked at last.

The doctor glanced at Farquart, who nodded his head.

"Yes, a roll of adhesive tape, a very big roll that had been lying on a table near the door."

"Adhesive tape?" The Chief Inspector raised an eyebrow.

"They use it to hold up the chins . . . to keep the mouth from opening," Sorensen explained. "Postmortem beauty treatment," he added with a sardonic smile.

"That's all?"

"Yes."

"What about the corpse in the dissecting laboratory? Was it dressed?"

"No. But in this case . . . oh, Gregory's already told you the whole story, hasn't he?"

"I forgot to mention it before . . ." the lieutenant cut in quickly, experiencing an unpleasant sensation because his memory lapse had been discovered. "The body wasn't dressed, but the janitor claims he was short one doctor's coat and two pairs of white pants—the kind the students wear in the summertime. A few pairs of disposable slippers may have been missing also, but the janitor says he never manages to keep an accurate count on them—he says the cleaning woman steals a few every once in a while."

The Chief Inspector took a deep breath and tapped on the desk with his eyeglasses.

"Thank you. Doctor Sciss, may I trouble you now?"

Without stirring from his casual position, Sciss muttered incoherently and finished writing something in an open notebook which he was supporting on his sharp, protruding knee.

Then, bending his balding, somewhat birdlike head, Sciss slammed the book closed and slipped it under his chair, pursed his thin lips as if he wanted to whistle, and stood up, rubbing his fingers against his twisted, arthritic joints.

"I consider your invitation to be a useful *novum*," he said in a high, almost falsetto voice. "It so happens that I generally tend to sound like a lecturer. I hope none of you mind; in any event it's quite unavoidable. Now then, I have made a thorough study of this series of incidents. As we have seen, the classical methods of investigation—the collection of evidence and the search for motives—have failed completely. Consequently, I have utilized the statistical method of investigation. It offers obvious advantages. We can often define a crime at the scene of its occurrence by the kinds of facts that are connected with it and the kinds that are not. For example, the shape of the bloodstains found near a murdered body may have a connection with the crime, and if so they can say a good deal about the way it was committed. Certain other facts, however—for example, that a cumulus or cirrostratus cloud floated over the scene of the crime on the day of a particular homicide, or that the telephone wires in front of the house where the crime took place are made of aluminum or copper—can be classified as nonessential. As far as our series of incidents is concerned, it is altogether impossible to decide in advance

15

which of the facts accompanying the incidents were connected with the crime and which were not.

"If it were only a matter of one incident," Sciss continued, "we would be at an impasse. Fortunately, however, there were several incidents. Now it stands to reason that a virtually unlimited number of objects and phenomena could have been found or observed in the vicinity of the incidents during the critical period. Therefore, to prepare a useful statistical series, we must rely only on those facts that are common to all the incidents, or at any rate, to a substantial majority of the incidents. Thus, we proceed by preparing a statistical breakdown of all the phenomena. Until now this method has almost never been used in a criminal investigation, and I am very pleased that I now have an opportunity to introduce it to you gentlemen, together with my preliminary findings. . . ."

Dr. Sciss, who until now had been standing behind his armchair as if it were a lectern, took a few steps in the direction of the door, turned unexpectedly, inclined his head, and continued, looking into the room at the seated men.

"Now, let us begin. First, you will recall that before any of these phenomena occurred there was a temporary phase which we can label conventionally as the 'forerunner stage.' During this stage bodies changed positions. Some turned upside down. Others were found on their sides. Still others were found on the floor next to their coffins.

"Second, with only one exception, each corpse belonged to someone who had died in his prime.

"Third, in each incident, again with one exception, some kind of covering was provided for the body. Twice this was ordinary clothing. Once it was most likely a doctor's coat and white trousers, and once—a black cloth curtain.

"Fourth, none of the corpses involved had been autopsied; all were undamaged; all were well preserved. Furthermore, every incident took place within thirty hours of the time of death, a fact particularly worthy of your attention.

"Finally, all the incidents, again with one exception, took place in small town mortuaries to which entrance is usually quite easy. The only disappearance that doesn't fit this pattern is the one at the Medical School."

Sciss turned to the Chief Inspector.

"I need a powerful spotlight. Can you get something for me?"

The Chief Inspector said a few quiet words into the intercom. During the ensuing silence, Sciss opened his spacious, bellowslike leather briefcase and slowly drew out a sheet of tracing paper, folded several times and covered with colored markings. Gregory looked at it with a mixture of aversion and curiosity. The scientist's patronizing attitude irritated him. Stubbing out his cigarette, he tried unsuccessfully to guess what was written on the paper rustling in Sciss's awkward hands.

Meanwhile, tearing one side of the paper slightly as he worked, Sciss unfolded it and spread it out on the desk in front of the Chief Inspector, whom he hardly seemed to notice, then walked over to the window and looked out at the street, holding one wrist with the fingers of the other hand as if checking his own pulse rate.

The door opened; a policeman came in with an aluminum spotlight on a high tripod and connected it to an outlet. Sciss switched it on. Waiting until the door had closed behind the policeman, he focused a bright circle of light on the huge wall map of England, then placed the sheet of tracing paper over it. Unfortunately, it was impossible to see the map through the translucent paper, so he moved the spotlight away, took the map down from the wall (swaying precariously on a chair to do so), and clumsily hung it on a stand which he pulled from a corner to the middle of the room. The spotlight was set up again where it could shine through the map from behind, while Sciss, with his arms spread wide to hold the sheet of tracing paper open, moved in front of it. This position—with outstretched, raised arms —was obviously uncomfortable beyond description.

Sciss finally managed to steady the stand with his leg. Holding the tracing paper from the top, he turned his head sideways.

"Please direct your attention to the area in which our incidents have occurred," he said.

Sciss's voice was more high-pitched than before, possibly because he was trying not to show how much he was exerting himself.

"The first disappearance took place in Treakhill on January sixteenth. Please remember the places and dates. The second—January twenty-third, in Spittoon. The third— February second, in Lovering. The fourth, February twelfth, in Bromley. The most recent incident took place on March eighth in Lewes. If we treat the location of the first incident as the starting point, and enclose it in a circle with an expanding radius, the results are as shown by the notations on my tracing paper."

A section of southern England along the Channel coast was clearly demarcated by the powerful beam of light. Five concentric circles encompassed five towns, each marked by a red cross. The first cross appeared in the center, the others were much closer to the perimeter of the largest circle.

Watching for signs of fatigue in Sciss, whose arms, still outstretched to hold the tracing paper, were not even trembling, Gregory began to feel tired.

"If you want me to," Sciss said in a shrill voice, "I will explain my calculations later on. Right now I shall only give you the results. The incidents occurred in a particular sequence: the more recently each incident took place, the farther it is located from the center—that is, from the site of the first disappearance. In addition, there is another significant item: the time between the respective incidents, counting from the first one, gets longer and longer, although not as if they were in proportion to each other in some specific ratio. But if temperature is also taken into account, it becomes evident that there is a certain regularity. More specifically, the product obtained by multiplying the time elapsed between any two incidents, and the distance separating any two consecutive disappearing-body sites from the center, when multiplied by the differential between the prevailing temperatures at both sites . . .

"This gives us," Sciss continued after a moment, "a constant of five to nine centimeters per second and degree. I say five to nine because the exact time of disappearance was not ascertained in any of the incidents. Therefore, in each case we have to deal with a broad, multi-houred time block during the night, or, more precisely, during the latter half of the night. If we take a mean of seven centimeters as the true quantity of the constant, and then do certain calculations, which I have already completed, we get a rather curious result. The causal factor of these phenomena, which have been moving steadily from the center toward the perimeter, does not lie in Treakhill at all, but has shifted westward to the towns of Tunbridge Wells, Engender, and Dipper . . . that is, the very places where there were rumors circulating about moving corpses. If, on the other hand, we attempt an experiment based on a completely accurate location point to determine the geometric center of the phenomena, we find that it is not located in any of the mortuaries, but about eighteen miles southwest of Shaltam—in the moors and wastelands of Chinchess. . . ."

Inspector Farquart, whose neck had been turning progressively more red as he listened to all this, was finally unable to contain himself.

"Are you trying to tell us," he exploded, "that an invisible spirit of some kind came up out of those damned moors, flew through the air, and snatched the bodies?"

Sciss began to roll up his paper. Standing in the glow of the hidden spotlight, thin and dark against the bright greenish map behind him, he resembled a bird more than ever (a swamp bird, Gregory thought to himself). Sciss carefully hid the tracing paper in his battered old briefcase and straightened up. He looked coldly at Farquart, his face covered with red blotches.

"I have nothing to add beyond the results of my statistical analysis," he declared. "A close relationship can easily be demonstrated between eggs, bacon, and the stomach, to name only one example, or a distant relationship, with somewhat more difficulty, between, for example, a country's political system and its average marital age. But regardless of the degree of difficulty, there is always a definite correlation, a valid basis for a discussion of causes and effects."

With a big, carefully folded handkerchief, Sciss wiped several droplets of sweat from his upper lip. Replacing it in his pocket, he continued.

"This series of incidents is hard enough to explain, and preconceived notions of any kind must be avoided. If you insist on displaying your prejudices to make things difficult for me, I will be forced to give up the case, as well as my cooperation with the Yard."

Sciss waited a minute, as if hoping someone would pick up the challenge, then walked over to the wall and turned off the portable spotlight. The room became almost completely dark. Searching for the light switch, Sciss momentarily moved his hand along the wall.

In the brightness of the ceiling light the room's appearance changed. It seemed to become smaller, and for a second the Chief Inspector, with his dazed, blinking eyes, reminded Gregory of his old uncle.

Sciss returned to the map.

"When I began my study," he continued, "so much time had already elapsed since the first two incidents, or rather, to be completely accurate, so little attention had been given to the incidents in the local police blotters and so few facts recorded, that it was impossible to reconstruct a detailed, hour-by-hour record of what happened. Because of this I limited myself to the remaining three incidents. In all three cases, I discovered, it was foggy—thick fog in two instances, extremely thick fog in the other. Moreover, several vehicles are known to have passed within a radius of several hundred yards of the site of each incident. Granted, none of the reports mentioned any 'suspicious' vehicles, but it's hard to say what the criteria for suspiciousness could possibly have been. Certainly no one would have driven to the scene of the crime in a truck marked 'Body Snatchers Ltd.,' but a vehicle could have been parked not too far from the scene, if necessary. Finally, I learned that around twilight of the evening preceding the night of each of the disappearances . . ." Sciss paused, then went on in a quiet but distinct voice, "some kind of domestic animal was observed close to the scene—and was reported either as a type of animal not usually found in a mortuary, or as one which my informants didn't recognize or had never seen before. In two cases it was a cat and once it was a dog."

A short laugh, transformed immediately into a poor imitation of a cough, resounded through the room. It came from Sorensen. Farquart sat absolutely still, not responding even to Sciss's rather questionable joke about "suspicious" vehicles.

Gregory noticed the Chief Inspector glaring in Sorensen's direction and immediately understood its significance: not a reprimand, not even anger, but a clear-cut and inescapable expression of authority.

The doctor coughed again to save face. Complete silence

followed. Sciss stared through the window over their heads at the increasing darkness outside.

"To all appearances, the statistical significance of the last fact is not very great," he finally continued, lapsing more and more frequently into a falsetto. "I ascertained, however, that stray dogs and cats are almost never found roaming around the mortuaries in which the incidents took place. Furthermore, one of the reported animals—the dog, to be specific—was found dead four days after one of the disappearances. Taking all this into account, I decided to offer a reward for anyone uncovering the corpse of the cat that was seen in connection with the last incident. This morning I received some news which cost me fifteen shillings. Some schoolchildren found the cat buried in the snow near a clump of bushes less than two hundred paces from the mortuary."

With his back to the others, Sciss walked over to the window as if he wanted to go outside. It was already too dark to see anything except for the street lights wobbling in the wind and glimmering in the swaying shadow of an overhanging branch.

He stood silently, stroking the lapel of his baggy gray jacket with the tips of his fingers.

"Are you finished, Doctor?"

Sciss turned around at the sound of Chief Inspector Sheppard's voice. A slight, almost boyish smile unexpectedly changed his small face, in which all the features were completely out of proportion, with its gray eyes, somewhat puffy cheeks, and a jaw so recessive that he was practically chinless.

Why he's only a boy at heart . . . a perpetual adolescent, really quite pleasant in his way, Gregory thought in amazement.

"I'd like to say a few more words, but not until the end of the meeting," Sciss replied, returning to his seat.

22

The Chief Inspector removed his eyeglasses. His eyes were tired.

"Good. Farquart, please, if you have anything else to say."

Farquart answered without much enthusiasm.

"Truthfully, not very much. I've gone over this whole 'series,' as Dr. Sciss calls it, in the usual way, and I think at least some of the rumors must have been true. It seems to me that the case is fairly simple—the perpetrator wanted to steal a corpse but was frightened away in Shaltam and the other places. He finally succeeded in Treakhill, but since he was still an amateur he took a naked body. It looks like he didn't realize how hard it would be to transport a body in that condition, as opposed to a fully clothed body, which is much less conspicuous. He must finally have realized this because he changed his tactics, making a definite effort to get clothing for the bodies. Also, the bodies he took the first few times weren't exactly the best available—I'm thinking about what Dr. Sciss called the search for bodies 'in good condition.' For example, there was another body in the mortuary at Treakhill—a young man's body—in much better condition than the one that disappeared. That's about all. . . .

"Of course there's still the question of motive," Farquart continued after a moment. "I see the following possibilities: necrophilia, some other kind of insanity, or some kind of . . . scientist. I think we should find out what Dr. Sorensen has to say about it."

"I'm not a psychologist or a psychiatrist," the doctor sputtered in a gruff voice, "but you can absolutely rule out the possibility of necrophilia. Necrophiliacs are always feebleminded, retarded cretins who couldn't possibly plan anything as complicated as this. In my opinion you can also rule out any other kind of insanity. Nothing was left to chance in any of these incidents. There's too much precision, not a single slipup of any kind. Madmen don't operate so methodically."

"Paranoia?" Gregory suggested in a low voice. The doctor glanced at him indifferently. For a moment he seemed to be trying the feel of the word on his tongue, then he pursed his thin, froglike lips.

"No! At least," he added, weakening the categorical character of his objection, "I don't think it's very likely. Insanity, gentlemen, is not a catchall for every human action that involves motives we don't understand. Insanity has its own structure, its own internal logic. Of course in the final analysis it's possible that the culprit could be a psychopath —yes, it's possible, I suppose—but it's only one of many possibilities."

"A psychopath with a talent for mathematics," Sciss commented almost involuntarily.

"How do you meant that?"

Sorensen turned to Sciss with a foolish but distinctly offensive sneer.

"I mean a psychopath who decided to have his fun by making sure that the product of the distance and the time between consecutive incidents, multiplied by the temperature differential, would be a constant."

Sorensen stroked his knee nervously, then began drumming on it with his fingers.

"Yes, yes I know . . . you can multiply and divide almost anything by something else—the length of canes by the width of hats—and come up with all kinds of constants and variables."

"Are you trying to make fun of mathematics?" Sciss began. It was clear that he was about to say something nasty.

"Excuse me, Doctor, but I would very much like to hear your opinion about the third possible motive." Sheppard was glaring at Sorensen again.

24

"That the culprit is a scientist who steals bodies? No, absolutely not! Never in the world! The whole idea is ridiculous. The only scientists who steal cadavers for their experiments are in third-rate movies. Why steal a cadaver when it's easy enough to get one from any morgue, or even to buy one from the next of kin. Besides, scientists don't work alone anymore, and even if one had stolen a cadaver, although God alone knows why he would, he wouldn't be able to hide it from his colleagues and co-workers. You can safely eliminate that as a motive."

"In your opinion then," Sheppard said, "do we have anything to go on?" The Chief Inspector's ascetic face was expressionless. Gregory caught himself staring almost impertinently at his superior, as if studying a painting. Is he really like that, he wondered, is all this no more than a dull routine for him?

Gregory mused in this vein during the oppressive, unpleasant silence that followed the Chief Inspector's question. Again a far-off engine resounded in the darkness beyond the window: the deep rumble moved upward, then grew silent. The panes shook.

"A psychopath or nothing," said Dr. Sciss all of a sudden. He smiled and, indeed, seemed to be in a good mood. "As Dr. Sorensen so intelligently pointed out, psychopathic behavior is usually very distinctive—it is characterized by impulsiveness, stupidity, and errors due to an attention span limited by emotional disorder. Thus, we are left with nothing. Ergo, gentlemen, it is quite obvious that these incidents couldn't possibly have taken place."

"You're joking, I suppose," Sorensen growled.

"Gentlemen," Sheppard interrupted. "The amazing thing is that the press has been very easy on us so far, probably because of the war in the Near East. For the time being we haven't had to worry about public opinion, but we're going to hear plenty of criticism of the Yard before long. And so, at least as far as its formal aspects are concerned, the investigation must be expedited. I want to know exactly what has been done already and, in particular, what steps have been taken to recover the bodies."

"That's all the lieutenant's responsibility," said Farquart. "We gave him full powers two weeks ago, and since then he's been completely on his own."

Gregory nodded his assent, pretending not to have heard the criticism implicit in Farquart's words.

"Starting with the third incident," he said, "we began to take extreme measures. Immediately after a missing body was reported, we closed off the whole area within a radius of fifty miles, using all the local forces, highway and airport patrols, plus two squads of radio cars from the London tactical headquarters at Chichester. We set up roadblocks at every intersection, railroad grade crossing, tollgate, highway exit, and dead-end street . . . but nothing came of it. By coincidence we happened to pick up five people who were wanted on various other charges, but as far as our own problem is concerned we didn't accomplish anything. Of course it's not easy to close off an area that big, and from the practical standpoint you can never set up a net that's one hundred percent tight—it's always possible for someone to slip through. After the second and third incidents the perpetrator probably left the area before our roadblocks were even set up, since he had six hours the first time and about five hours the next. I'm assuming, of course, that he also managed to dispose of his car. In the most recent incident, however, the disappearance took place between 3:00 and 4:50 in the morning, so he didn't have more than an hour and three quarters for his escape. It was a typical March night . . . gale winds and snow after an evening of thick fog, and all the roads were impassable until noon of the next day. Of course the perpetrator might have used a tractor or a snowplow to make his getaway, but it would have been hard, and I know this from my own experience because we had an awful time getting our patrol cars out of the snow, both the ones from the local stations and the ones from the Greater London C.I.D. reserve that responded to our alert."

"So you maintain that no car could have left the Lewes vicinity until noon of the next day?"

"Right."

"What about sledges?"

"Technically it would have been possible, but not in the amount of time he had to work with. After all, a sledge can't travel at more than a mile or two an hour, especially in a storm like the one they had that night. Even with the best horses he wouldn't have been able to get out of the closed-off area by noon."

"If you say so, Lieutenant, but a moment ago you told us that this kind of net isn't completely secure," Sheppard said gently. "In fact, an absolutely secure cordon is only an ideal we aspire to."

"Besides," Farquart commented, "he could have put the corpse in a bag and carried it through the fields on foot."

"Impossible," said Gregory. He wanted to remain silent but his cheeks were burning. He could hardly keep himself from jumping to his feet.

"No vehicles left the closed-off zone after six in the morning. I can vouch for that," he declared. "Maybe an infantryman could have gotten through the snow but not with a load as heavy as an adult body. He would have dumped it. . . ."

"Maybe he did dump it," Sorensen observed.

"I thought of that, but we combed the whole area—there was a thaw the next day which made the job easier—and we didn't find a thing."

"Your reasoning is hardly as faultless as you think," Sciss unexpectedly broke into the conversation. "First of all, you didn't find the dead cat, but if you had really conducted a careful search you would have—"

"Excuse me," said Gregory, "but we were looking for a human corpse, not for a dead cat."

"Exactly! But there are so many places to hide a corpse in such a large area that you might just as well conclude that it isn't there."

"The perpetrator could have buried the body," Farquart added.

"He snatched it just to bury it?" Gregory asked with an innocent air. Farquart snorted.

"Maybe he buried it when he saw he couldn't get away."

"But how did he know he couldn't get away? After all, we weren't announcing the roadblocks on the radio," Gregory retorted. "That is . . . unless he has a contact in the department, or unless he's a police officer. . . ."

"That's not a bad thought," Sciss smiled. "But in any case, gentlemen, you haven't exhausted all the possibilities. What about a helicopter?"

"What nonsense!" said Dr. Sorensen contemptuously.

"Why? There aren't any helicopters in England?"

"The doctor apparently believes that it's easier to suspect a psychopath than a helicopter," said Gregory, smiling complacently.

"What about all the carcasses?" Sorensen added.

There wasn't a sound from Sciss, who seemed to be absorbed in his lecture notes.

"The search for the bodies must be continued," Sheppard went on. "We have to plan a much more comprehensive operation, including ports and dockyards. Some kind of surveillance of ships and cargoes. Do any of you have anything else to say? Any new ideas? Any theories? Anything at all? Please don't be afraid to be outspoken, even too outspoken."

"In my opinion, it's not possible—" Gregory and Farquart began at the same time. They looked at each other and stopped.

"I'm listening."

No one spoke. The telephone jangled. The Chief Inspector disconnected it and watched the men seated before him. A cloud of bluish tobacco smoke rose around the lamp. For a moment, silence reigned.

"In that case, I . . ." Sciss said. He was meticulously folding his manuscript and putting it into the briefcase. ". . . I have applied the constant which I explained to you earlier in order to determine the sequence and location of these phenomena in advance."

He stood up, moved over to the map, and, using a red pencil, marked off an area encompassing part of the counties of Sussex and Kent.

"If the next incident takes place between tomorrow morning and the end of next week, it will occur in this sector, which is bounded on the north by the suburbs of East Wickham, Croydon, and Surbiton, on the west by Horsham, on the south by a strip of the Channel coast, and on the east by Ashford."

"A pretty big area," Farquart said dubiously.

"Not really, since we can exclude an interior sector in which incidents have already taken place. The phenomenon is characterized by its movement outward, so the only area actually involved is a circular strip no more than twenty-one miles wide. It includes eighteen hospitals and about one hundred sixty small cemeteries. That's all."

"And you . . . you're sure there will be an incident in this area?" asked Sorensen.

"No," Sciss replied, after hesitating for a rather long moment, "I'm not sure. But supposing it doesn't take place . . . or, rather, that if it doesn't take place . . ."

Something curious was happening to the scientist. Everyone watched in amazement as he began shaking and his voice started to crack like an adolescent boy's. Suddenly Sciss burst out laughing. He roared with laughter as if delighted by some private thought, totally oblivious to the deadly silence with which his uncontrollable hilarity was greeted.

Sciss picked up his briefcase from under the armchair, nodded his head in a slight bow, and, his shoulders still heaving spasmodically, walked out of the office, taking quick, inordinately long steps.

2.

A strong wind scattered the clouds, and the yellowish glow of the setting sun became visible above the rooftops. The street lights dimmed, the snow darkened and blended into the sidewalks and gutters. His hands in his coat pockets, Gregory walked quickly, not looking into any of the doorways he passed.

Hesitating for a moment at an intersection, he shifted his weight from one foot to the other, shivering in the cold, damp air. Finally, angered by his own indecisiveness, he turned to the left.

The meeting had ended—in fact, dissolved—immediately after Sciss's dramatic exit. Nothing had been accomplished. Sheppard hadn't even decided who was going to take over the case. Since he had only seen him five or six times before, Gregory hardly knew the Chief Inspector. Of course he was aware of all the usual methods for bringing oneself to the attention of a superior officer, but he had never resorted to such tactics during his short career as a detective; now, though, he was beginning to regret this, because his relatively low rank reduced his chances of being put in charge of the investigation.

Sheppard had stopped Gregory just as he was leaving the conference room and asked him how he would conduct the investigation. Gregory had answered that he didn't know. The truth, of course, but honest answers usually don't pay. Sheppard would probably regard Gregory's response as a sign that he wasn't too smart, or that he had a poor attitude.

And what had Farquart told the Chief about him, he wondered. Surely nothing very impressive. Gregory tried to reassure himself with the thought that he was just overrating Farquart by worrying this way, since Farquart's opinion really wasn't worth anything.

His thoughts wandered from Farquart's rather dull personality to Sciss. Now there was a character! Gregory had heard a lot about him.

During the war Sciss had been in the Operations Section, working close to the chief of staff, and from all accounts he had some pretty solid achievements to his credit. About a year after the war, though, he'd been fired. The story was that he'd insulted some VIP—it might have been Field Marshal Alexander—and the story was certainly believable. Sciss was well-known for his ability to antagonize everyone around him. It was also said that Sciss was standoffish, nasty, absolutely devoid of tact, and as unmercifully frank as a child in telling other people his opinions of them.

Remembering his own dismay at the meeting because he hadn't been able to counter Sciss's seemingly perfect logic, Gregory could well understand the animosity which the scientist seemed to inspire wherever he went. At the same time, though, he respected the intellectual powers of this strange man, whose tiny head made him resemble a bird. "I'll have to get busy on this," he said to himself, bringing his deliberations to an end, but without any clear sense of what "get busy" actually meant.

The day faded quickly, so quickly that the displays in the shop windows were soon being lit up for the evening. The street narrowed. Gregory found himself in a district of the city which hadn't been rebuilt since the Middle Ages. It was jammed with dark, clumsy old buildings, most of them sheltering brand-new modern shops that sparkled unnaturally like transparent glass boxes.

Gregory turned into an arcade, amazed that the thin layer of windswept snow at its entrance still hadn't been trampled. A woman in a red hat stood nearby looking at some smiling wax manikins dressed in evening gowns. Beyond her, where some square white floodlights brightened the concrete walk, the arcade curved slightly.

Walking slowly, hardly conscious of his surroundings and whereabouts, Gregory brooded about Sciss's laugh. What exactly had it meant, he wondered. It had to be significant. Despite appearances, Sciss didn't just do things for effect, although he was certainly arrogant enough, and consequently it followed that Sciss must have had a good reason for laughing, even if he was the only one who knew it.

Farther up the deserted arcade a man was walking toward Gregory—a tall, lean man, whose head was nodding as if he were talking to himself. Gregory was too busy with his own thoughts to pay much attention to him, but he kept him in sight out of the corner of his eye. The man drew nearer. Three shops turned off their lights for the night and the arcade suddenly became darker. The windows of a fourth shop were covered with whitewash because of a renovation in progress, and the only lights still visible were a few glittering displays in the direction from which the man was approaching.

Gregory looked up. The man's pace slowed, but he kept coming, albeit hesitantly. Suddenly they stood facing each other, no more than a few paces apart. Still engrossed in his thoughts, Gregory stared at the tall male figure before him without really seeing his face. He took a step; the man did the same.

"What does he want?" Gregory wondered. The two men scowled at each other. In the shadows the man's broad face was hidden; he was wearing his hat pushed down on his forehead, his coat was somewhat too short, and his belt was all askew, with its end twisted loosely around the buckle. There was certainly something wrong with the buckle,

Gregory thought, but he had enough problems without worrying about that too. He moved as if to walk past the stranger but found his path blocked.

"Hey," Gregory began angrily, "what the . . ." his words faltering into silence.

The stranger . . . was himself. He was standing in front of a huge mirrored wall marking the end of the arcade. He had mistakenly walked into a glass-roofed dead end.

Unable to escape the disconcerting feeling that he was really looking at someone else, Gregory stared at his own reflection for a moment. The face that looked back at him was swarthy, not very intelligent, perhaps, but with a strong, square jaw that showed firmness, or at least so he liked to think, although more than once he had decided it was only pigheadedness.

"Had a good look?" he muttered to himself, then turned on his heels in embarrassment and headed in the direction he had come from.

Halfway up the arcade, Gregory couldn't resist an irrational impulse to turn and look back. The "stranger" stopped also. He was far away now among some brightly lit, empty shops, heading down the arcade, busy with his own affairs in his mirror world. Gregory angrily adjusted his belt in its buckle, pushed his hat farther back on his head, and went out into the street.

The next arcade led him straight to the Europa. The doorman opened the glass door for him, and Gregory strode past the tables toward the purple glare of the bar. He was so tall that he had no trouble seating himself on one of the high stools.

"White Horse?" asked the bartender. Gregory nodded.

The bottle tinkled as if there were a glass bell hidden inside it. Gregory drank quickly. The White Horse was acrid; it tasted something like fuel oil and burned his throat . . . he hated it. It so happened, however, that several times in a row he had stopped at the Europa with Kinsey, a young colleague at the Yard, and each time he'd had a drink of White Horse with him; from then on the bartender had considered Gregory a regular customer and made a point of remembering his preferences. Actually, Gregory had only been meeting with Kinsey in order to put the finishing touches on an apartment exchange. He really preferred warm beer to whiskey, but was ashamed to order it in such a fashionable place.

Gregory had ended up at the Europa now simply because he didn't feel like going home. Meditating over the shot glass, he decided to see if he could organize all the facts of the "series" in some kind of systematic pattern, but found that he couldn't remember a single name or date.

He downed his drink, tilting his head back with an exaggerated gesture.

He flinched. The bartender was saying something to him.

"What? What did you say?"

"Do you want supper? We have venison today, it's in season."

"Venison?"

He couldn't understand a word the bartender was saying.

"Oh, supper," it finally dawned on him. "No. Please pour me another."

The bartender nodded. He rinsed out the glass at a silver-colored tap, rattling the faucets as if he wanted to smash them into little pieces, then raised his reddened, hard, muscular face to Gregory, and, watching through beady eyes, whispered.

"Are you looking for a—?"

There was no one else near the bar.

"No. What the hell are you talking about?" Gregory added indignantly, as if that had been his real purpose and he'd been caught in the act.

"No, nothing. I thought that you . . . for service," the

bartender mumbled, withdrawing to the other end of the bar. Someone touched Gregory's arm lightly. He whirled around in a flash and was unable to hide his disappointment: it was a waiter.

"Pardon me . . . Lieutenant Gregory? Telephone for you, sir."

Walking as quickly as possible to avoid being jostled, Gregory made his way through the crowd on the dance floor. The light in the telephone booth was burned out, so he stood in darkness, except when an occasional flash from the revolving light over the bar streamed through the booth's little round window.

"Hello, Gregory speaking."

"This is Sheppard."

At the sound of the Chief's far-off voice, Gregory's heart began to beat faster.

"Lieutenant, I want to see you."

"Of course, Chief Inspector. When should I . . ."

"I'd rather not put it off. Do you have time?"

"Naturally, yes sir. Tomorrow?"

"No. Today, if you can. Can you make it?"

"Yes sir, of course."

"That's fine. Do you know where I live?"

"No, but I can—"

"Eighty-five Walham Street, in Paddington. Can you come over now?"

"Yes."

"Perhaps you'd rather come in an hour or two."

"No, I can come now."

"All right, I'm expecting you."

The receiver jangled when Gregory hung up. He stared at the telephone in confusion. How in God's name did Sheppard know he was at the Europa, a place he only went to occasionally to find an outlet for his penny-ante snobbism.

Had the Chief been so eager to find him that he'd systematically phoned around from bar to bar? The very thought made Gregory turn red. He walked out into the street and ran to catch a passing bus. From the bus stop it was a long walk. He chose a roundabout route through back streets where there weren't too many people. Finally he found himself on a deserted side street lined by small old houses. Here and there a puddle shimmered in the light of the antiquated gas lamps illuminating the street. Gregory had never imagined there was such a seedy little neighborhood buried in the middle of this part of the city.

He was surprised again at number 85. In a garden behind a low brick wall, at a considerable distance from any of the other houses, there stood a massive building. It was completely dark, as if dead. Taking a good look around, Gregory finally spotted a weak glow coming from one of the upstairs windows.

The spiked gate made a creaking sound when he swung it open. Forced to grope in the darkness to get his bearings because the brick wall cut off the light from the street, Gregory used the tip of his foot to feel his way along a flagstone walk to the solid black door of the house. Instead of a bell there was a knocker. He pulled it gently as if afraid to make too much noise.

He had a long wait, occasionally hearing the dripping of an unseen rainspout or the sound of a car whizzing by on the wet pavement at the intersection. Finally, and soundlessly, the door opened. Sheppard was standing in the doorway.

"You're here already? That's fine. Please follow me."

The hall was completely dark. Farther inside the house, a weak glow streaked the stairs in a trail of light, beckoning upward. An open door on the second floor landing led into a small foyer. Gregory noticed something staring at him from overhead—it was the skull of some kind of animal, its looming, empty eye sockets clearly standing out from the yellowed bone.

He took off his coat and entered the room. The long walk in the fog had irritated his eyes and they still burned a little.

"Please sit down."

The room was almost dark. There was a lamp on the desk, but it was pointed downward toward an open book, its light reflected onto the wall and ceiling from the flattened pages. Gregory remained on his feet. There was only one chair.

"Please sit down," the Chief Inspector said a second time. It sounded like an order. The lieutenant sat down reluctantly. He was now so close to the source of the light that he was almost unable to see. A few blurred spots that were actually pictures were barely visible on the walls; under his feet he felt a deep rug. Opposite him was a long bookshelf. A television set glistened in the middle of a dull whitish area.

Sheppard walked over to the desk, pulled a black metal cigarette box out from under some books, and slid it over to his guest. He lit one himself and began pacing back and forth between the door and the window, which was screened by a heavy brown drape. The silence lasted so long that Gregory, who had nothing to do but watch the pacing figure, soon began to feel bored.

"I've decided to give you the case," Sheppard said all of a sudden, not losing a step.

Gregory didn't know what to say. He could feel the alcohol in him and took a deep drag on the cigarette as if tobacco smoke would restore his sobriety.

"You'll be on your own," Sheppard continued in a decisive tone of voice. Still pacing back and forth, he glanced obliquely at the figure seated in the circle of light next to the lamp.

"Don't think I picked you because you have any special ability as an investigator, because you don't. Furthermore, your methods are completely unsystematic. But it doesn't make any difference. You have a great personal interest in this case, don't you?"

"Yes," Gregory answered. He sensed that an uncomplicated affirmative reply would be best.

"Do you have any theories of your own about it? Something personal that you didn't want to mention in my office today?"

"No. That is . . ." Gregory hesitated.

"Go on."

"This is just an impression. It's not based on anything," said Gregory. He spoke with some reluctance. "But it seems to me that this case really isn't about bodies. I mean, they play a definite role, but not in this thing."

"In what thing?"

"I'm not sure."

"Really?"

The Chief Inspector sounded almost cheerful. Gregory wished he could see his face. This was a completely different Sheppard from the one he'd occasionally met at the Yard.

"In my opinion this is a lousy case," Gregory suddenly blurted out as if talking to a friend. "There's something about it . . . something peculiar. It's not that it's difficult, but there are details that don't fit . . . not for material reasons but because the only connecting links are all psychological nonsense. It all builds up to nothing and leads to a dead end. . . ."

"Yes, go on," Sheppard chimed in attentively, still pacing back and forth. Gregory was no longer watching him. Unable to tear his eyes from the papers on the desk, he began speaking excitedly.

"The idea that this whole case is based on some kind of

insanity, mania, or psychopathology is almost irresistible. No matter where you start, no matter how anxious you are to avoid it, everything leads you back to it. But as a matter of fact that's our out, because it only seems that way. All right, let's say it was a maniac. But everything was so carefully planned and methodical. . . . I don't know, do you see what I mean? If you went into a house and found that all the tables and chairs had only one leg, you'd probably tell yourself that it was the work of a madman, that some maniac had decided to furnish his house that way. But if you went from house to house and found the same thing all over town? I don't know what any of this means, but it just couldn't be . . . this is not the work of a madman. I think we have to go to the other extreme. Someone very intelligent who is using his intellect for a purpose we don't understand yet."

"What else?" Sheppard asked quietly, as if he didn't want to do anything to intrude on the fervor which had quite obviously seized Gregory. Sitting behind the desk, still staring blindly at the papers, the younger man was silent for a moment, then answered.

"What else? . . . Nothing very good. Nothing very good at all. A series of acts without a single slipup, that's pretty bad. . . . In fact it appalls me, it's absolutely inhuman. Human beings don't work that way. Human beings make mistakes, it's in the nature of things that they miscalculate from time to time, make mistakes, leave clues behind, change their plans in the middle of everything. But from the very beginning these bodies . . . the ones that were moved . . . if that's the right word for it . . . I don't agree with Farquart that the perpetrator ran away because he was frightened. It wasn't anything like that. At the time all he wanted was to move them. Just a little at first. Then a little more. Then, still more . . . until finally a body disappeared altogether. That's the way it had to be, that's the way he wanted to do it. I thought . . . I'm always thinking about it, why he . . . but I don't know. Nothing."

"Are you familiar with the Lapeyrot case?" Sheppard asked. Standing in the back of the room he was almost invisible.

"Lapeyrot? The Frenchman who—"

"Yes. In 1909. Do you know the case?"

"It sounds familiar, but I can't remember. What was it about?"

"About too much evidence. At least that's what they said at the time, unfortunately. On a beach along the Seine River, for a certain period, they kept finding buttons of various kinds arranged in geometric patterns, as well as belt buckles, suspender clasps, and small coins. Always arranged in polygons, circles, or other shapes. There were also handkerchiefs knotted together."

"Wait a minute. I remember something now. I must have read about it somewhere. Two old guys in a garret who . . . right?"

"Right. That's the very case I'm talking about. . . ."

"They used to search out young people who were trying to kill themselves—they'd bring them home, revive them, cheer them up, and have them tell what it was that had driven them to attempt suicide. That's the way it was, right? And after all that . . . they strangled them to death. Right?"

"More or less. One of the pair was a pharmacist. After the murders they got rid of their victims with the aid of some acid and a fireplace; then they'd amuse themselves by playing a little game with the police with the buttons, buckles, coins, and other odds and ends that were left over."

"I don't see the connection. One of the Lapeyrot murderers was insane. He completely dominated his accomplice, who was regarded as a victim of *folie à deux*. The two of

41

them devoted most of their energy to the button puzzles because that's what really excited them. The case may have been hard to crack, but basically it was quite commonplace: there were murderers and victims, there were clues. What difference does it make if the crime was committed with a few theatrical flourishes—"

Gregory stopped short, an incomprehensible smile suddenly appearing on his lips. He looked at the Chief Inspector, trying to get a glimpse of him in the dim light.

"Wait, I think I see . . ." he said, his tone indicating that he had just made a startling discovery. "So that's it."

"Yes, that's it exactly," Sheppard answered, resuming his pacing.

Gregory bowed his head, tapping on the edge of the desk with his fingers.

"Theatrical," he whispered. "An imitation . . . but an imitation of what?" he said, raising his voice. "A sham, but to cover what? Insanity? No, it can't be anything like that. The circle is closing again."

"It's closing because you're going in the wrong direction. When you talk about shammed insanity you're looking for a close analogy to the Lapeyrot case, in which the murderers, if I may put it this way, had a particular audience in mind all along: they purposely left clues to give the police a puzzle to solve. In our case there's nothing to indicate that any of this is aimed at the police. In fact, I doubt it very much."

"Yes, well in that . . ." said Gregory. He felt downhearted and stifled. "So we're back where we started. The motive."

"No, not at all. Look over here, please."

Sheppard pointed to the wall, at a small circle of light that Gregory hadn't noticed before. Where was it coming from, he wondered. Glancing at the desk, he saw a cut-glass paperweight standing next to the reflector of the desk lamp; a narrow beam of light, refracted in its crystalline depths, was escaping into the room's dark interior to shine on the wall.

"What do you see here?" asked Sheppard, moving to the side.

Gregory leaned over to escape the lamp's blinding glare. There was a picture hanging on the wall, almost invisible in the darkness except for one of its corners, which was lit by the single beam of light. Within this tiny space, not much larger than two coins placed side by side, he saw a dark spot enclosed by a pale gray, slightly curved border.

"That spot?" he asked. "A profile of some kind? No, I can't make it out . . . wait a minute. . . ."

Intrigued by the shape, Gregory studied it more and more carefully, his eyes squinting. The more he studied it the more anxious he became. Although he hadn't the slightest idea what he was looking at, his anxiety began to increase.

"It looks as if it's alive . . ." he said involuntarily in a low voice. "Is it a burned-out window in a gutted house?"

Sheppard moved closer to the wall and blocked the area with his body. The irregular spot of light now shined on his chest.

"You can't figure it out because all you can see is a tiny part of the whole," he said, "right?"

"So that's it! You think these disappearing body incidents are only a part—let's say the beginning—of something bigger."

"That's it exactly."

Sheppard was pacing again. Gregory returned his gaze to the spot on the wall.

"It may even be the beginning of something with criminal and political implications that go beyond the boundaries of this country. What comes next, of course, will depend on what has already taken place, and naturally it could all work out differently. Maybe everything that's happened so far is only a diversion, or camouflage for some other operation. . . ."

Deeply engrossed in the dark, nerve-wracking shape, Gregory hardly heard him.

"Excuse me, Chief Inspector," he interrupted. "What is that thing?"

"What? Oh, that."

Sheppard switched on the ceiling light and the room was filled with brightness. A second or so later he switched it off again, but during the few instants of light Gregory finally managed to catch a glimpse of what he had been staring at so fruitlessly: it was a woman's head thrown backward at an angle, the whites of her eyes staring straight ahead, her neck scarred by the mark of a noose. There wasn't enough time for him to see all the details, but even so, with a peculiar kind of delayed action, the expression of horror in the dead face got to him, and he turned to Sheppard, who was still pacing back and forth.

"Maybe you're right," said Gregory, blinking his eyes, "but I don't know if that's the most important thing about it. Do you really believe that a man alone in a darkened mortuary in the middle of the night would tear apart a cloth curtain with his teeth?"

"Don't you?" Sheppard interrupted.

"Yes, of course, if he did it because he was nervous or afraid, or if there weren't any other tools available . . . but you know as well as I do why he did it. That damned iron-clad consistency that we've seen throughout this whole series. After all, he did everything to make it look like the bodies had come back to life. He planned everything to achieve that effect, even studied the weather reports. But how could he possibly predict that the police would be ready to believe in miracles? And that's exactly what makes the whole thing so insane!"

"The kind of criminal you're talking about doesn't exist

and couldn't possibly exist," Sheppard observed indifferently. He pushed the drapes to the side and looked out a dark window.

After a long interval Gregory asked, "Why did you bring up the Lapeyrot case?"

"Because it began childishly, with buttons arranged in patterns. But that isn't the only reason. Tell me something: exactly what is contrary to human nature?"

"I don't understand . . ." Gregory mumbled. He was beginning to get a splitting headache.

"A person manifests his individuality by his actions," the Chief Inspector explained quietly. "Naturally this holds true for criminal acts also. But the pattern that emerges from our series of incidents is impersonal. Impersonal, like a natural law of some kind. Do you see what I mean?"

"I think so," said Gregory. His voice was hoarse. He leaned over to one side, very slowly, until he was completely out of the blinding glare of the desk lamp. Thanks to this movement his eyes were soon able to see better in the darkness. There were several other pictures hanging next to the photograph of the woman, all showing the faces of dead people. Meanwhile, Sheppard had resumed his pacing across the room, moving back and forth against a background of nightmarish faces as if he were in the middle of some kind of weird stage setting; no . . . more as if he were among very ordinary, familiar things. He paused opposite the desk.

"The mathematical perfection of this series suggests that there is no culprit. That may astound you, Gregory, but it's true. . . ."

"What . . . what are you . . ." the lieutenant gasped in a barely audible voice, recoiling involuntarily.

Sheppard stood absolutely still, his face unseen. Suddenly Gregory heard a short, quavering sound. The Chief Inspector was laughing.

"Did I shock you?" the Chief Inspector asked in a more serious tone. "Do you think I'm talking nonsense?

"Who makes day and night?" he continued. There was derision in his voice.

Suddenly Gregory stood up, pushing his chair backward.

"I understand," he said. "Of course. The series has something to do with the creation of a new myth. An imitation of one of the laws of nature. A synthetic, impersonal, invisible, obviously all-powerful criminal. Oh, it's perfect! An imitation of infinity . . ."

Gregory laughed, but not very happily. Then, breathing deeply, he became quiet.

"Why are you laughing?" the Chief Inspector asked gravely, perhaps even a bit sadly. "Isn't it because you were already thinking along the same lines but rejected the idea? Imitation? Of course. But a perfect imitation, Gregory, so perfect that you'll come back to me with your hands empty."

"Maybe," Gregory said coldly. "And in that case I'll be replaced by someone else. If necessary I could manage to explain every detail right now. Even the dissecting laboratory. The window can be opened from the outside with the aid of a nylon thread looped around the lock beforehand. I tried it, and it works. But to think that the creator of a new religion of some kind, an imitator of miracles, had to begin this way . . ."

Gregory shrugged his shoulders.

"No, it can't be that simple," the Chief Inspector said. "You keep repeating the word 'imitation.' A wax doll is an imitation of a human being, isn't it? What if someone made a doll that could walk and talk, wouldn't that be an excellent imitation? And if he made a doll that could bleed? A doll that could experience unhappiness and death, what then?"

"And what does any of this have to . . . after all, even

the most perfect imitation—even the doll you were just talking about—has to have a creator, and the creator can be held responsible!" Gregory shouted, overcome with anger. "He's only playing with me" suddenly flashed through his mind, and he said, "Chief Inspector, please answer one question for me."

Sheppard looked at him.

"You don't really think this case can be solved, do you?"

"Certainly not. I don't want to hear that kind of talk anymore. Of course there is a possibility that the solution—" The Chief Inspector broke off in mid-sentence.

"Please, sir, tell me everything."

"I don't know if I have the right," Sheppard said dryly, as if displeased by Gregory's insistence. "You might not like the solution."

"Why? Please, explain it to me a little more clearly."

Sheppard shook his head.

"I can't."

He walked over to the desk, opened the drawer, and removed a small package.

"Let's work on the part that pertains to us," he said, handing it to Gregory.

The package contained photographs of three men and one woman. Commonplace, banal faces, indifferent to everything, stared at Gregory from the shiny little cardboards.

"That's them," he said, recognizing two of the photos.

"Yes."

"Don't you have any pictures taken after death?"

"I managed to get two." Sheppard reached into the drawer. They had been taken at the hospital at the request of the families.

Both photographs were pictures of men. And it was a strange thing: death seemed to give a new dignity to their rather ordinary features, bestowing a kind of motionless gravity upon them. Dead they looked more expressive than

47

they had while living, as if they finally had something to hide!

Gregory looked up at Sheppard. To his surprise, the Chief Inspector was hunched over, suddenly looking much older than before. He was clenching his lips as if in pain.

"Chief Inspector?" he said softly, with unexpected timidity.

"I would prefer not to give this case to you . . . but I have no one else," said Sheppard in a quiet voice. He placed his hand on Gregory's shoulder. "Please keep in touch with me. I'd like to help you, although I have no idea whether my experience will have much value in a case like this."

Gregory drew back and the Chief Inspector's hand dropped. Both men were now standing outside the circle of light made by the lamp, and in the darkness the faces on the wall stared down at them. The lieutenant felt more drunk than he had all evening.

"Please sir . . ." he said, "you know more than you're willing to tell me, don't you?" He was a bit breathless, as if he'd been exerting himself strenuously.

"Sir . . . are you unwilling to tell me, or unable?" Gregory asked. He wasn't even shocked at his own audacity.

Sheppard shook his head in denial, watching Gregory with a look of immeasurable patience. Or was it irony?

Gregory glanced down at his hands and noticed that he was still holding the photographs, the ones of the live subjects in his left hands, the dead ones in his right. And again he was inspired by the same mysterious compulsion that had made him direct such an odd question to the Chief Inspector. It was as if an invisible hand was touching him.

"Which of these are . . . more important?" he asked in a barely audible voice. It was only possible to hear him because the room was absolutely still.

A tight-lipped expression on his face, Sheppard made a discouraging gesture and went over to the light switch. The room was flooded with brightness, everything became ordinary and natural. Gregory slowly hid the photographs in his pocket.

The visit was obviously coming to an end. During the remainder of their conversation, which concentrated on such concrete matters as the number and posting of the constables guarding the mortuaries, the organization of a cordon around the areas mentioned by Sciss, and the details of the lieutenant's actual powers, there remained the shadow of something left unsaid.

Again and again the Chief Inspector would fall silent and look at Gregory anxiously, as if uncertain whether to leave these businesslike considerations and resume the previous conversation. But he left well enough alone and didn't say anything.

Gregory was halfway down the stairs when the lights went out. He managed to feel his way to the door. Suddenly he heard his name.

"Good luck!" the Chief Inspector shouted after him.

The lieutenant walked out into the wind and closed the door.

It was terribly cold. The puddles had all solidified; frozen mud crunched underfoot; in the onrushing wind the drizzling rain was being changed into a blizzard of icy needles that pricked Gregory's face painfully and made a sharp, paperlike rustle as they bounced off the stiff fabric of his coat.

Gregory tried to review the details of the evening, but he might just as well have tried to classify the invisible clouds that the wind was driving around over his head. Remembered snatches of this and that struggled in his mind, spilling over into images unconnected with anything except a poignant feeling of depression and being lost. The walls of the room had been covered with posthumous photographs, the desk with open books, and he vehemently regretted now

49

that he hadn't taken a good look at any of them, or at the papers spread out next to the books. It never even occurred to him that such actions would have been indiscreet. Gregory began to feel that he was standing on the boundary between the definite and the indefinite. Each of his thoughts seemed about to reveal one of many possible meanings, then vanished, melting away with every desperate effort he made to grasp it fully. And he, pursuing understanding, seemed about to plunge into a sea of ambiguous details in which he would drown, comprehending nothing even at the end.

Whom was he supposed to catch for Sheppard—the creator of some new religion? Although able to function smoothly and efficiently in routine cases, the machinery of investigation was now beginning to turn against itself. The more meticulously the facts were measured, photographed, recorded, and assembled, the more the whole structure seemed to be nonsensical.

If he'd been asked to track down a completely obscure and unknown murderer, Gregory wouldn't have felt so helpless. What, he wondered, was that confused anxiety he had seen in the eyes of the old Chief Inspector, who wanted to help him but couldn't?

Furthermore, why had the Chief, who seemed to think the case was unsolvable, picked him, a beginner, to take it over? And was that really the reason Sheppard had invited him to his house in the middle of the night?

With his fists clenched in his pockets, Gregory walked along the deserted street, not seeing anything in the darkness, not feeling the raindrops trickling down his face, not remembering where he was headed for. He gulped in some of the cold, damp air and again saw Sheppard's face before him, the little shadows at the corner of his mouth twitching.

How long was it since he had left the Europa? He began to calculate. It was now 10:30, so nearly three hours had gone by. "I'm not drunk anymore," he said to himself. Stopping in the circle of light around a lamp post, he read the street sign to get his bearings, figured out the location of the nearest subway station, and headed toward it.

The streets became more crowded, brightened now by neon signs and by blinking red and green traffic signals. Once inside the revolving doors at the subway entrance, Gregory was met by a blast of warm, dry air from the heating ducts. He rode downward on the escalator, slowly sinking into the noisy rumbling below.

It was even warmer on the station platform than it had been upstairs. Gregory let the Islington train pass, watching the triangular red light on the last car until it disappeared in the distance. Circling around a newsstand, he leaned against an iron support beam and lit a cigarette.

After a while his train arrived. The doors opened with a pneumatic hiss. Gregory took a corner seat. The car jerked and pulled out, the station lights flicking by more and more quickly, then disappearing; the train was soon moving so fast that the lights in the tunnel couldn't be distinguished from each other as they shot past.

Staring blankly at the row of accidental faces sitting opposite him, Gregory again reviewed the meeting with Sheppard. There was more to it than he yet understood, he felt, but he'd only be able to figure out its real meaning if he concentrated.

Gradually he became aware of an uneasy feeling circulating in his consciousness, and finally it formed itself into words: "There's trouble. Something terrible and irreversible happened this evening . . . or was it today?" As if cut off by some outside force, this line of thought suddenly came to a dead end.

Gregory closed his eyes for a moment. Suddenly it occurred to him that he had recognized a man sitting at the opposite end of the car, near the door. He took another look. Yes, the face was familiar all right. It seemed eager to tell him something. Gregory tried to concentrate. It was an old man's face: flabby, with vague, spongy features.

The man was fast asleep, his head propped up against a partition, his hat slowly slipping downward and casting a deep shadow across his face. His body rocked back and forth with the movements of the speeding train, the rhythm intensifying on the curves. After one particularly sharp jolt, the man's big, pale, swollen hand slipped out of his lap, as if it were a bundle, and dangled lifelessly at his side.

Gregory was sure he knew the sleeping man, but as much as he tried he couldn't place him. The train moved faster and faster, the jolting increased, and finally the man's lower jaw dropped open. The lips fell apart. . . .

"He's sleeping as soundly as a corpse," flashed through Gregory's mind. At the same moment he was overcome by a cold, terrifying sensation. For an instant he couldn't catch his breath. He knew. The sleeping man was the subject of one of the posthumous photographs in his coat pocket.

The train came to a stop. Cross Row. A few people got on. The platform lights started to flicker, seemed to move, then whisked away backward. The train sped on.

Brilliantly lit signs and advertising posters were soon flashing by again. Although it was nearly time for him to get off, Gregory didn't even bother to glance at the station sign. He sat absolutely still, as if concentrating deeply, his eyes focused on the sleeping man. The doors closed with a hiss; outside the windows a horizontal row of shining fluorescent lights flowed smoothly backward, suddenly disappearing as if slashed away. Steadily picking up speed, the train raced into the dark tunnel.

Gregory's head began to throb. Oblivious to the noisy clatter of the wheels, he began to feel as if he was looking at the sleeping man's head through a long, gray funnel filled with flashing sparks. The dark, gaping mouth hypnotized him; he stared so steadily, so unmovingly, so fixedly, that the swollen gray face seemed to transform itself into a circle of iridescent light. Keeping his eyes fixed on the old man, Gregory reached into his coat, unbuttoning it to pull out the photograph. The train hissed to a stop. Where were they? Camberwell already?

Several people rose to get off. A soldier, making his way to the door of the car, tripped over the extended leg of the sleeping man, who suddenly woke up and, without a word, adjusted his hat, arose from his seat, and joined the exiting crowd.

Gregory jumped up, attracting attention by his haste. Several faces turned in his direction. The doors began to close. Forcibly holding them open, Gregory leaped onto the platform from the moving train. Running along the platform, he caught a glimpse of an angry face against the background of the moving cars. "Hey you!" the train dispatcher shouted after him.

A cool breeze met Gregory's nostrils. He stopped abruptly, his heart beating with excitement. Along with the rest of the crowd, the man was making his way toward a tall iron exit gate. Gregory drew back and waited. Behind him was a newsstand lit by the strong light of a single naked bulb.

The old man had a game leg. He was limping along slightly behind the crowd of passengers. With the brim of his hat soaking wet and flopping about soggily, his creased coat frayed around the pockets, he looked like the last of the old-time panhandlers. Gregory glanced at the photograph hidden in his palm. There was no resemblance.

He lost his head completely. Was this just an accidental case of mistaken identity, or was it due to his confused state of mind? The dead man was much too young; he couldn't possibly be the person he'd followed off the train.

Confused and feeling somewhat nearsighted, his cheeks twitching, Gregory looked alternately at the photo and at the old man, whose unshaven gray face sagged over his collar. Finally sensing that he was being watched, the old man turned toward the detective. Having no idea why the latter was so interested in him, his face took on an empty-headed, listless expression, his slack jaw dropped slightly, his slobbering lips parted, and as a result he suddenly seemed to resemble the man in the photograph again.

Gregory extended his hand as if to touch the old man's shoulder. The old man, terrified, cried out—or, more accurately, uttered a hoarse, frightened sound—and hurried onto the escalator.

Just as Gregory set off in pursuit, a family with two children stepped between him and the old man, blocking his way. Seeing this, the old man slipped through the other passengers and was carried farther and farther upward.

Gregory shoved his way through the crowd of people blocking his path, paying no attention when an indignant woman said something nasty and a few other angry remarks were directed his way. On the street-exit level the crowd was so thick that he couldn't get through and finally had to give up, letting himself be carried along at the slow pace imposed by the others. There wasn't a sign of the old man when he finally reached the street. Looking helplessly in all directions, Gregory berated himself for that split second of hesitation—due either to surprise or to fear—in which the old man had made his escape.

The traffic was heavy on both sides of the safety island where he had emerged from the subway. Blinded by the headlights every time he tried to cross, Gregory stood helplessly at the curb. Before long a taxi pulled up, the driver assuming that he was waiting for a cab. The door opened. Gregory got in and mechanically uttered his address. When the taxi began moving he noticed that he was still clutching the photograph in his hand.

About ten minutes later the taxi came to a stop at the corner of a small street just off Odd Square. Gregory got out, already half-convinced that he had experienced a hallucination of some kind. Sighing, he stuck a hand in his pocket and fumbled for his keys.

The house in which he lived was owned by the Fenshawes. It was an old, two-story building, with an entrance portal almost monumental enough for a cathedral; a steep, gabled roof; thick, dark walls; long hallways abounding in sudden turns and hidden alcoves; and rooms so high they seemed to have been designed for some kind of flying creature. This suggestion was reinforced by the extraordinary wealth of ornamentation on the ceilings. With its high gilded vaults in a constant state of semidarkness due to an effort to save electricity, its broad marble staircases, wide-columned terrace, mirrored drawing room with chandeliers copied from those of Versailles, and its huge bathroom (which was probably once a parlor)—the house had a strange splendor, and it was this that had fired Gregory's imagination when, accompanied by his new colleague, Kinsey, he had first seen it.

And since the Fenshawes had made a good impression on him, he decided to take his colleague's advice and rent the room, which Kinsey was giving up, or so he said, for personal reasons.

Unfortunately, the Victorian architects who designed the house hadn't known anything about modern home appliances, and as a result the place presented a number of inconveniences. To get to the bathroom Gregory had to walk the length of a long hallway and through a glassed-in gallery; to get to his room from the stairs he had to pass through a six-doored drawing room which was almost unfurnished, not counting a few blackening bas-reliefs on the peeling walls, a crystal chandelier, and the mirrors in each of its six corners. After a while, though, the house's defects didn't seem too serious.

Since he led a very busy life, returning home late at night and spending the whole day at work, it was a long time before Gregory noticed how peculiar his new residence was; nor did he realize, at first, how much he was being drawn into its orbit.

The Fenshawes were well on in years, but growing old gracefully. Pale and thin, with colorless, slightly graying hair, Mr. Fenshawe was a melancholy man who, because his nose looked as if it had been borrowed from a different, considerably more fleshy face, gave the impression of being in disguise. He favored old-fashioned clothing, usually wore brilliantly polished shoes and a gray frock coat, and, even at home, always carried a long cane. His wife was a dumpy woman with small, dark, shining eyes. She walked around in dark dresses that bulged strangely (after a while Gregory began to suspect that she was puffing herself out on purpose), and she was so taciturn that it was difficult to remember the sound of her voice. When Gregory asked Kinsey about the owners, the answer had been, "Don't worry, you'll get along with them," followed, a moment later, by, "They're such riffraff." At the time Gregory had only wanted some support for his decision to move into the big, old house, so he didn't pay much attention to this mysterious remark, the more so because he was accustomed to Kinsey's penchant for bizarre expressions.

The morning after he moved in Gregory encountered Mrs. Fenshawe for the first time. It was quite early. Striding along on his way to the bathroom, he came upon her in the drawing room. She was sitting on a low stool that looked as if it had been made for a child, a rag clutched in one hand, some kind of sharpened metal implement in the other.

Using her feet to hold back a section of carpet, she was buffing the parquet flooring, working her way along the length of the room, but making such slow progress that she had moved less than two feet by the time Gregory came back from the bathroom, finding her as busy and preoccupied as before. In the middle of the huge drawing room, she looked like the black head of a slowly contracting caterpillar whose body was formed by the patterned rug. When Gregory asked if he could help with anything, Mrs. Fenshawe turned her leathery face in his direction for a moment but didn't say a word. That afternoon, on his way out of the house, Gregory tripped over her as she was moving from step to step on her little stool (the lights were off), nearly knocking her down the stairs. From time to time thereafter he ran into her in the most unlikely and unexpected places, and when he was working in his room he sometimes heard the slow, measured creaking of her stool as she made her way along the hall. Once, when the creaking stopped just opposite his door, he assumed, with some distaste, that his landlady was spying on him through the keyhole. He quickly stepped into the hall, but Mrs. Fenshawe, who was fastidiously polishing the parquet under the window, ignored him completely.

Gregory concluded from all this that Mrs. Fenshawe was trying to save money by cutting down on domestic help; she used the stool because it was uncomfortable for her to bend over. This explanation, though presumably correct, did not eliminate the problem, however, because the constant sight of Mrs. Fenshawe creeping along on her stool, and the perpetual creaking from dawn to dusk, soon took on a demonic character in Gregory's mind. He began to yearn for the moment when the creaking would stop; sometimes he had to wait an hour or two to get some peace. Moreover, Mrs. Fenshawe was usually accompanied by two black cats, which to all appearances she took care of, and Gregory, for no apparent reason, couldn't stand either of them. At least a dozen times he told himself that none of this was any of his business, and in fact if it hadn't been for Mr. Fenshawe he would have been able to ignore everything that went on outside his room.

Although the old man's room was right next door to his and shared the same beautiful terrace, Gregory never heard a sound from Mr. Fenshawe in the daytime. The nights were a different story. Well after ten o'clock, sometimes not until after eleven, Gregory would hear a rhythmic knocking from behind the wall separating the two rooms. Sometimes it was a rich, sonorous sound; sometimes hollow and dull, like someone tapping on a wooden wall with a hammer. This was usually followed by several other acoustical phenomena. At first it seemed to Gregory as if these came in an infinite number of variations, but he was wrong, and within a month he was able to recognize the eight most frequent sounds.

The initial knocking behind the wall was usually followed by a dull, empty noise, rather like the sound of a small barrel or a piece of wooden pipe being rolled along a bare floor. Sometimes there were some quick vigorous thumps on the floor, as if someone were walking barefoot with his full weight on his heels. Other times there was clapping—heavy, mean-sounding slaps like those an empty hand might make against a moist balloon-like surface filled with air. There was an intermittent hissing sound also and, finally, some faint noises that were difficult to describe. A persistent scraping, interrupted by a metallic rapping, then by a sharp flat whack like the sound of a fly swatter, or like the tightly wound string of a musical instrument being snapped.

These sounds followed each other in no particular order, and, with the exception of the soft thumps, which Gregory characterized to himself as barefoot stomping, some of them might even be missing for several evenings in a row. Always performed with a certain amount of technical finesse, the sounds increased steadily in tempo, and once they began one could always look forward to a serenade of the most unusual richness and pitch. The sounds and murmurs were usually not very powerful, but to Gregory, lying under his cover in a dark room and staring at a high, invisible ceiling, it sometimes seemed as if they were loud enough to shatter his brain, and in time his interest in the sounds changed from simple curiosity to an almost pathological obsession, although, since he didn't go in for self-analysis, he would have been hard put to say just when this change took place. It may be that Mrs. Fenshawe's peculiar behavior during the daytime made him oversensitive to the miseries he had to endure every night. At the beginning, though, he was so busy with a case that he couldn't worry very much about all this, and in any event, because he was so busy he slept well and hardly heard anything. After several nights of the noises, however, his dark room began to feel like an echo chamber. Gregory tried to convince himself that Mr. Fenshawe's nocturnal activities were none of his business, but by then it was too late.

Next Gregory tried rationalizing. Faced with a collection of weird, incomprehensible sounds that no one ever mentioned, he attempted to work out a logical explanation of some kind that would cover everything. This, he soon discovered, was impossible.

Where once he had always slept like a log, dropping off as soon as he hit the sheets, and listening to the complaints of insomniacs with a polite attitude that verged on disbelief, now, in the Fenshawe house, he began to take sleeping pills.

Every week, Gregory had Sunday dinner with his landlords. The invitation was always extended to him on the preceding Saturday. On one of these occasions he managed to sneak a look into Mr. Fenshawe's bedroom, but he regretted this immediately because what he saw exploded his elaborately constructed theory that his landlord was conducting a complicated scientific experiment. Except for a huge bed, a chest of drawers, a night table, a sink, and two chairs, the bright triangular room was empty. There wasn't a sign of tools, wooden boards, balloons, metal containers, or kegs. There weren't even any books.

The Sunday dinners were usually quite dull. The Fenshawes were conventional people who lifted their convictions and opinions from the pages of the *Daily Chronicle*; they rarely had anything original to say, and their conversation generally centered on repairs the old house needed and the difficulty of raising money to pay for these, along with a few anecdotes about some distant relatives in India who apparently comprised the more exciting branch of the family. All this was so trite and commonplace that any mention of the night sounds, or of Mrs. Fenshawe's processions around the house on her stool, would have been out of place; in any event, whether or not this was actually so, Gregory could never quite manage to say anything about these matters.

Afterward, Gregory would tell himself that it was a waste of time to worry about any of this: if he could only think the matter through, or at least formulate a reasonable theory about what his neighbor was doing behind their mutual wall in the middle of the night, he told himself, he would finally be free from the agonizing hours of tossing sleeplessly in a dark, lonely room.

But the idea of making sense out of a series of weird, disjointed sounds floated around in Gregory's head as if in a void. Once, somewhat groggy from a sleeping pill which had made him drowsy without bringing rest, he quietly slipped out of bed and went out on the terrace, but the glass doors to Mr. Fenshawe's room were covered from the inside with a heavy, nontransparent curtain. Gregory returned to his room shivering from the cold and, feeling like a whipped

60

dog, he slipped under the covers, overcome with gloom because he had tried to do something for which he would always be ashamed.

Gregory's work kept him so busy that he rarely thought about the noises during the daytime. At most, he was reminded of them once or twice when he bumped into Kinsey at Headquarters. On these occasions Kinsey always eyed him expectantly, with an air of cautious curiosity, but Gregory decided not to bother him about it. After all, in the long run the problem was trivial. In time, perhaps without even realizing it, Gregory gradually began to change his routine: he brought official reports home and brooded over them until midnight, sometimes even later. This enabled him to lie to himself about the ultimate disgrace that was already so close, for during his long hours of sleeplessness, the most extraordinary ideas were coming into his head, and several times he had conceived a desperate desire to just give up and take refuge in a hotel or a boardinghouse.

This evening more than ever, returning from Sheppard's, Gregory needed peace and quiet. The alcohol had worked its way out of his system long before, although he still felt angry and had a pungent taste in his mouth, and his eyes smarted painfully as if there were sand beneath the lids. The staircase, immersed in darkness, was deserted. Gregory passed quickly through the drawing room, where the dark mirrors glistened coldly in the corners, and closed the door of his room with a sigh of relief. Out of habit—it had already become almost a reflex—he stood perfectly still for a moment, listening. At such times he didn't think; his behavior was instinctive. The house was as still as death. Gregory turned on a lamp, noticed that the air in the room was heavy and stuffy and flung open the door to the terrace, then set about making coffee in his little electric pot. He had a splitting headache. Earlier in the evening other things had distracted him, but now the pain came up to the surface of his consciousness and demanded his full attention. He sat down on a chair next to the bubbling pot, but the feeling that he had just gone through a lousy, unlucky day was so inescapable that he had to stand up. Relax, he told himself, nothing really awful had happened. He'd been given the slip by a man on the subway who vaguely resembled one of the missing corpses. Sheppard had put him in charge of the very investigation he wanted to command. True, the Chief had babbled strangely for a while, but in the end it was all only words, and Sheppard was certainly entitled to carry on if he wanted to. Maybe he was getting religious in his old age. What else had happened? Gregory reminded himself of the incident in the dead-end arcade—the meeting with himself —and laughed involuntarily. "That's the detective in me. . . . Ultimately, even if I bungle this case, nothing will happen," he thought. He took a thick notebook out of his drawer, turned to a blank page, and began writing: "MO-TIVES: Greed. Religious Fervor. Sex. Politics. Insanity."

Glancing back at what he had written, Gregory crossed out each item on the list except "Religious Fervor." What a ridiculous idea! He threw the notebook aside and leaned forward, resting his head in his hands. The pot was bubbling viciously now. Maybe his silly little list of motives wasn't so stupid after all, he reflected. A frightening idea began to work its way to the surface. Gregory waited passively, gloomily beginning to feel like a struggling, helpless insect trapped in an incomprehensible darkness.

Shivering, he got up, walked over to his desk, and opened a bulky volume entitled *Forensic Medicine* to a place indicated by a bookmark stuck between the pages. The chapter heading read, "The Decomposition and Decay of the Corpse."

He began reading, but after a while, although his eyes obediently continued to follow the text, his mind began to visualize Sheppard's room with its gallery of dead faces. He pictured the scene: Sheppard pacing back and forth in an empty house, stopping occasionally to take a look at the pictures on the wall. Shivering again, Gregory made a decision: Sheppard was a prime suspect. Suddenly he heard a shrill whistle and realized that the coffee was ready.

Closing the book, Gregory got up, poured himself a cup, and gulped it down while standing at the open door of the terrace, not even noticing that the hot coffee was burning his throat. A hazy glow hung over the city. He could see far-off cars shooting along the nighttime streets, looking, in the distance, like white flashes disappearing into a black abyss. From inside the house there was a faint rustling. It sounded a little like a mouse eating its way through the wall, but Gregory knew it wasn't. Feeling as if he had lost even before the game really started, Gregory ran out on the terrace. Supporting himself on the stone balustrade, he raised his eyes upward. The sky was full of stars.

3,

That night Gregory had a dream in which everything became crystal clear and he cracked the case, but in the morning he couldn't remember a single detail. Part of it came back to him while he was shaving. He was at a shooting gallery in Luna Park firing a big red pistol at a bear. He'd just scored a bull's-eye when the bear growled and reared up on its hind legs; suddenly it wasn't a bear at all but Doctor Sciss, very pale and wrapped in a dark cloak. When Gregory took aim, the pistol became as soft as a piece of rubber. He kept pressing his finger against the place where there should have been a trigger even though it didn't do any good. That was all he could remember. When he finished shaving, he decided to phone Sciss and arrange a meeting. On his way out of the house he saw Mrs. Fenshawe in the hall, rolling up a long carpet runner. One of the cats was curled up under her stool. Gregory could never tell the cats apart, although he could see the differences between them when they were together. After a quick breakfast in a cafeteria on the other side of the square, he telephoned Sciss. A woman's voice at the other end told him that Sciss had left London for the day. This ruined Gregory's plan. Uncertain what to do next, he went out into the street, strolled around for a while gazing at the store windows, and then, for no reason at all, spent an hour wandering through Woolworth's. Around twelve o'clock he left Woolworth's and finally checked in at Scotland Yard.

It was Tuesday. Making a mental note of the number of days still remaining in the period Sciss had specified, Gregory skimmed through a sheaf of reports from the outlying suburbs, carefully went over the latest weather information and the long-range forecasts for southern England, chatted for a while with the typists, and arranged to see a film that evening with Kinsey.

After the film he was still at a loss for something to do. He most definitely did not want to spend any more time in his room studying *Forensic Medicine,* not from laziness but because the pictures always upset him, although naturally he'd never admit that to anyone. There was a long wait ahead; he knew it would pass more quickly if he could find an interesting diversion, but it wasn't easy. After killing some time by compiling a long list of books and old issues of *Archives of Criminology* to borrow from the department library someday, he went to his club to watch a soccer game on television, then read for a few hours at home, finally falling asleep with the feeling that the day had been a total waste.

The next morning Gregory made a resolution to learn something about statistics, and on his way to the Yard he picked up a few books on the subject. He hung around the Yard until dinner time. After eating, he found himself in the subway station at Kensington Gardens. Deciding to try amusing himself with a game he'd invented when he was a student, he got on the first train that came along, got off just as randomly when he felt like it, and for a whole hour rode haphazardly around the city.

This little game had always fascinated Gregory when he was nineteen. He used to stand in the middle of a crowd without knowing until the last minute whether or not he'd board an approaching train, waiting for some kind of internal sign or act of the will to tell him what to do. "No matter what I won't move from this spot," he would sometimes swear to himself, then would jump on just as the doors were shutting. Other times he would tell himself severely, "I'll take the next train," and instead would find himself entering the one standing right before him. The very concept of chance had fascinated Gregory when he was younger, and through self-analysis and research he had tried to study its workings in his own personality, though without any results, to be sure. Apparently such efforts to uncover the mysteries of the personality were somewhat more interesting when one was nineteen years old. Now, however, Gregory was forced to conclude that he had already become a completely different and much less imaginative person: at the end of an hour (having finally forced himself to change to the right train, even though he was quite aware that he had nothing else to do) he was bored again. Around six o'clock he stopped in at the Europa; seeing Farquart at the bar, however, he left at once before his colleague caught sight of him. He went to the movies again that evening and was bored stiff by the film. Later, he studied statistics texts in his room until he fell asleep while trying to work out an equation.

It was still dark when the ringing of the telephone awakened him and forced him out of bed.

Running barefoot along the cold parquet floor, Gregory realized that the ringing had begun as part of a dream. Half-asleep, unable to find the light switch, he groped for the receiver while the phone kept ringing insistently.

"Gregory speaking."

"It's about time! I was beginning to think you were spending the night with someone. Well, at least you can get a good night's sleep—we're not all that lucky. Listen! A report just came in. There was an attempted body snatching in Pickering."

Gregory recognized the voice as soon as he heard the first word: it was Allis, the duty officer at the Yard.

"Pickering? Pickering?" he tried to remember. He stood up, still a little unsteady on his feet from sleepiness, while the duty officer's shouting continued.

"The constable detailed to the mortuary wound up under a car. There's probably an ambulance there by now, but the story's all confused. The car that ran over the constable smashed into a tree. You'll find out the rest for yourself."

"When did all this happen? What time?"

"Oh, maybe half an hour ago. The report just came in. Do you want anyone special? Tell me now, because I'm sending a car out to pick you up."

"Is Dudley around?"

"No. He was on duty yesterday. Take Wilson. He's not any worse. You can pick him up on the way. I'll call him and get him out of bed."

"All right, let it be Wilson. And get me someone from the lab also. Thomas would be best of all, do you hear? Oh, what the hell, let's take the whole crew. And a doctor too. What about a doctor?"

"I already told you that they sent an ambulance. There's probably a doctor there by now."

"But I want one from the Yard, man, from the Yard! Not a healing doctor—just the opposite!"

"Right! I'll take care of it. But you'd better hurry. As soon as I hang up I'm going to send the car."

"Give me ten minutes."

Gregory switched on the lamp. In the darkness, when the phone began ringing, he felt a tingling excitement, but the feeling had disappeared without a trace when he heard the duty officer's first words. He ran to the window. It was still almost pitch-dark, but it had snowed during the night and the streets were covered with a layer of white. "Perfect," he said to himself. He ran on tiptoe to the bathroom, guessing there'd be enough time for a shower before Thomas managed to pack up all his junk, and he wasn't mistaken. When he walked out to the gate, wrapped in his raincoat with the collar pulled up around his neck, the car still hadn't arrived. He glanced at his watch: nearly six o'clock. A moment or so later he heard the sound of a motor. It was a big, black Oldsmobile. Sergeant Calls was sitting behind the wheel, next to him Wilson, the photographer, and in the back seat two other men. The car was still moving when Gregory jumped in, slamming the door behind him, and with a jerk it accelerated to full speed, its headlights glimmering brightly.

Gregory was jammed into the back seat with Sorensen and Thomas.

"Do you have anything to drink?" he asked.

"There's some coffee in a thermos next to the doctor," said Calls from behind the wheel. He was speeding through the deserted streets at nearly seventy miles per hour, his siren howling. Gregory found the thermos, drained a full cup in one gulp, and passed it on to the others. The siren wailed in the night. This was the kind of ride Gregory loved. The headlights swept around the turns. It was gray everywhere, except for the white snow in the street.

"What happened out there?" Gregory asked. No one answered.

"The report came in from the local station," said Calls after a moment.

"It seems that the guy on duty at the cemetery was pulled out from under a car by one of our motorcycle patrols. He had a broken head or something like that."

"I see. What about the bodies?"

"The bodies?" Calls repeated slowly. "I guess they stayed there."

"What do you mean 'stayed there'?" Gregory asked, a little taken aback.

From the other side of the back seat, Thomas, the technical man, added a comment. "It looks like they scared the guy and he ran away."

"We'll see about that," Gregory snarled. The Olds gave a loud roar as if it needed a new muffler. They were leaving the crowded buildings behind and approaching the suburbs. Near a big park they ran into a patch of fog. Calls slowed down, then stepped on the gas again when the fog cleared up. By the time they reached the outskirts of the city the traffic was beginning to get heavier: huge trailer trucks, brightly lit double-decker buses already crowded with commuters. Calls kept the siren blaring to clear the way.

"You didn't get any sleep tonight, did you?" Gregory said to the doctor. Sorensen had dark circles under his eyes. He was slumped forward like a cripple.

"I went to bed around two o'clock. It's always like this. And you can bet there won't be anything for me to do when we get there."

"We'd all rather be asleep," said Gregory philosophically.

They raced through Fulham, slowed down just before the bridge, and crossed the Thames in a light fog. Below them the river was the color of lead. Some kind of small boat was passing by and they could hear the sound of a foghorn in the distance. A moment later a clump of trees on the bridge abutment was flashing by. Calls drove with great care. In fact, in Gregory's opinion he was the Yard's best driver.

"Does the Chief know yet?" Gregory didn't direct the question to anyone in particular.

The answer came from Thomas, a short, vigorous man like the sergeant, but with a little mustache that made him look like a suburban hairdresser. "Yes, Allis was in touch with him. In fact, he gave all the orders."

Gregory leaned forward. He was more comfortable that way, and he enjoyed watching the road through the space between the shoulders of the two men in the front seat. Passing trucks had tamped the wet snow on the pavement into a smooth crust, and he loved the way Calls took the curves, braking at the last minute as he raced into the turn, then, halfway around, stepping down on the gas and barreling ahead at full speed. Of course Calls never took a turn on two wheels—that would have been bad form for a police driver, except, perhaps, in unusual circumstances—but in any case, in snow like this you could end up in a ditch that way.

They were past Wimbledon already; the speedometer, oscillating gently, reached ninety, inched on toward one hundred, moved slightly backward, and, with a jiggle, again advanced, the needle making small jumps between the graduated points on the face of the gauge. Suddenly there was a big Buick in front of them. Calls honked his horn, but the other driver didn't seem to hear. As they drew closer they could see a teddy bear dangling in the back window of the bright red sedan, and Gregory was reminded of the dream he'd had two days before. He smiled, experiencing a pleasant sense of strength and confidence.

Meanwhile, Calls caught up with the other car. When he was no more than fifteen feet behind it, he hit the switch and the siren emitted an earsplitting scream. The Buick braked violently, its rear wheels struggling for traction and splattering snow on their windshield; as it began to pull over the Buick skidded slightly in the deeper snow on the side of the road and its rear swung around toward the hood of the police car: a crash seemed inevitable, but Calls, giving the steering wheel a sharp, fast turn which threw them all to the right, speeded past. The shocked expression on the face of the young woman in the Buick remained with them even after they'd left the scene far behind. By the time it occurred to Gregory to look out the back window, she had managed to get back on the road again.

The fog began to lift and they found themselves in the middle of a snow-whitened plain. Here and there, almost vertical columns of smoke rose from the houses; the sky was so flat and still, so nondescript in color, that it was difficult to tell whether or not it was cloudy. Speeding through an interchange, their tires thumping nervously, they shot onto the expressway. Calls seemed to be drunk with power: crouching over the wheel, he pressed down even harder on the foot pedal; its engine roaring, the black sedan leaped forward at a hundred and ten miles per hour.

A town came into view in the distance, and Calls pulled over next to a road sign. Running off to the left of the expressway was a narrow road lined by a double row of old trees. About two hundred yards straight ahead, the expressway turned in the other direction. As soon as they stopped Gregory stood up—at least to the extent that standing was possible inside the car—and leaned forward to get a look at the map which the sergeant was spreading out on the wheel. They had to turn off to the left.

"Are we in Pickering yet?" asked Gregory. Calls was fiddling with the gearshift lever as if it were a toy.

"Another five miles."

They followed the side road up a gently sloping hill, passing two or three long, barracks-style wooden buildings. As they reached the top of the incline the sun came out; the air, washed by the fog, was clean and sparkling, and it began to feel warmer. The whole town was spread out below them, the smoke from its chimneys turning pink in the bright sunlight. A narrow stream cut through the snow, leaving a twisting dark trail.

They drove on, crossing a small concrete bridge. On the other side, the figure of a helmeted constable, his overcoat reaching almost to his ankles, loomed before them, a red stop-disk in his hand. Calls stopped the car and rolled down his window.

"From here on you have to walk," he informed his passengers, after exchanging a few words with the constable, then threw the car into gear and pulled over to the side of the road. They all got out. Everything seemed different now: white, quiet, peaceful; the first sign of the morning sun over the distant forest; the air crisp yet springlike. Globs of snow dropped onto the pavement from the overhanging branches of the chestnut trees along the road.

"Over there," the constable said, pointing to where the road, curving gently, swung around the next hill. They stepped off the road onto a narrow footpath lined by white bushes, at the end of which they could see a brick roof. About three hundred paces straight ahead, a wrecked car was barely visible in the dark shadow cast by the trees. With Gregory in the lead, they followed the roadside path as directed by the constable, the wet snow squishing unpleasantly under their feet and sticking to their shoes, and soon reached a section of road blocked off by ropes; behind the barrier some tire tracks stretched from the road to the shoulder, then swung across to the scene of the accident.

There, half on the road, half off, stood a long, gray Bentley, its front end rammed into a tree trunk, its headlights smashed to bits, its front windshield cracked. The doors were hanging open and, as much as Gregory could see, the inside of the car was empty. One of the local policemen walked over. Gregory continued studying the position of the Bentley and, without turning around, asked:

"Well, what happened?"

"The ambulance left already, Inspector. They took Williams," the constable answered.

"Williams—was he the one on duty at the mortuary?" Gregory turned to the constable.

"That's right, Inspector."

"I'm a lieutenant. Where is this mortuary?"

"Over there, sir."

Gregory glanced in the direction indicated. The cemetery was unwalled; its long, regular lines of graves were covered with snow. He hadn't noticed it before because it was located off to the east, and to see it he would have had to look right into the rising sun, which was still fairly low on the horizon. Nearby, hidden by a few bushes, a footpath branched off from the road and led up to a building surrounded by a thicket.

"Is that the mortuary? The building with the tar-paper roof?"

"Yes, Lieutenant. I was on duty there until three this morning, then Williams relieved me. The way it was, our commanding officer got us all together, because—"

"Slow down and tell me the whole story. Williams had the duty after you. What happened next?"

"I don't know, sir."

"Well, who does?"

Gregory was experienced with this kind of conversation, so he remained patient.

Meanwhile, after getting the lay of the land, the men from the Yard settled down to their work. The photographer and the lab technician dumped their gear in the snow near where the highway patrolman's motorcycle was leaning against the mile post. Sorensen tried to light a cigarette but his matches kept going out in the wind. The constable, a blonde, friendly-looking fellow with big eyes, cleared his throat.

"No one, Lieutenant. It was like this. Williams had the duty from three o'clock. Parrings was supposed to relieve him around six, but around half past five a driver called the station house to report that he'd just hit a constable who ran in front of his car, and that he smashed into a tree while trying to swerve out of the way. So then—"

"No," said Gregory, "not yet. Now, tell me slowly, very slowly. First, exactly what was the man on duty at the mortuary supposed to do?"

"Well . . . we were supposed to walk around the place and check the door and windows."

"All around the building?"

"Not exactly, sir, because there are bushes right up to the

wall in the back, so we made a wide circle up to the graves and back."

"How long did it take to make one circuit?"

"It depends. Tonight it took about ten minutes, because it was hard to get around in the snow and there was all that fog, and of course we had to check the door every time. . . ."

"Good. Now tell me, what about the driver who phoned the station?"

"Sir?"

"Where is he now?"

"The driver? At the station, sir. He had a slight cut on his head and Dr. Adams wanted to look him over."

"I see. Dr. Adams is the local doctor?"

"That's right, sir."

Still standing at the side of the road, Gregory suddenly snapped at the constable in an unexpectedly severe voice.

"What idiot was walking around in here and crushed all this snow? Was there anyone here you didn't tell me about?"

Surprised but unperturbed, the constable winced.

"No one, sir. The C.O. told us to rope off the whole area to make sure."

"What do you mean, no one? What about the ambulance crew? How did they get to Williams?"

"Oh, Williams was a little ways from here—we found him under that tree over there." The constable pointed across the road at a depression in the snow perhaps ten or twelve paces behind the Bentley.

Without another word, Gregory stepped over the rope and, keeping as much to the side as possible, walked across the closed-off area. Like their car, he noticed, the Bentley had come from the direction of London. Stepping carefully, he walked back and forth a few times following the tracks. The impression of the tires was clear and even up to a certain point; from there on the snow was scattered in small lumps and bare pavement was visible. Apparently the driver had braked violently and his wheels, skidding sideways, had acted something like a snowplow. Farther on, still visible in the snow, were some long curving tracks leading right up to the rear tires of the Bentley, showing that it had swung sideways and driven straight into the tree. The tracks of a few other cars were also still preserved in the wet, plastic snow, especially along the side of the road. Among these were some deep ruts apparently left by the thick tires of a heavy truck; the treads were arranged in a characteristic prewar style. Gregory walked back in the direction of London for a while, and without any difficulty ascertained that the Bentley was the last car to have driven along this section of road, since in a few places its tire tracks had obliterated the marks left by the other vehicles. Now he began to look for human footprints: he headed in the opposite direction, moving away from the men and cars; the footpath, he found, was covered with footprints: enough for there to have been a parade. It must have been the ambulance attendants carrying the injured constable, he realized, making a mental note to compliment the Pickering police commander for having kept them off the road. The only footprints on the road itself had been made by a pair of heavy boots. It was evident that they were the tracks of a running man; someone who was probably not too good at running, though, because he had taken very short steps, apparently in an amateurish effort to increase his speed.

"He ran from the direction of the cemetery out into the middle of the road," Gregory oriented himself, "and then headed toward the town. A constable running like that? Who was chasing him?"

He looked around for signs of the pursuer but there wasn't a thing: the snow was untouched. Walking farther on, Gregory came to the place where a narrow lane, surrounded by dense bushes, branched off from the road and went up to the cemetery. About twenty paces farther along the road beyond that point, he saw some tire tracks and footprints in the snow, untouched and preserved perfectly. A vehicle had driven up from the opposite direction, turned around, and stopped (the tire tracks at this point were more deeply grooved); two men had gotten out; a third had approached them from the side, and led them over to the Bentley. They had walked toward it along the shoulder and had come back the same way. The man they were carrying had probably given them a little trouble, because there were a few round marks in the snow to indicate where they had set the stretcher down before sliding it into the ambulance. The spot where he found all these prints was just past the beginning of the lane, so Gregory took a look at the lane next, returning to the road after a moment or two because he had seen what he wanted: the running man's tracks showed clearly how he had charged down the lane from the direction of the mortuary, the recently whitewashed wall of which blocked the view for about a hundred yards.

Carefully examining the running man's footprints, Gregory walked back to the Bentley. Eight paces from the wrecked car, the prints showed, he had whirled around, as if suddenly trying to turn; a bit farther on the snow was so churned up that there wasn't much to see. Standing with his hands in his pockets, Gregory bit his lip.

"He missed him in front, then went into a skid and hit him . . . probably with his rear end." Gregory lifted his head.

"How badly is Williams hurt?"

"He's still unconscious, sir. The doctor—the one from the ambulance—was very surprised that he managed to keep walking afterwards—he didn't fall down until he got over . . . oh, over here."

"How do you know that's where he collapsed?"

"Because there's some blood. . . ."

Gregory bent down and took a good look. Three, no four, coagulated brown spots had seeped so deeply into the snow that it was difficult to see them.

"Were you here when the ambulance took him away? Was he conscious?"

"Oh no, sir, definitely not!"

"Was he bleeding?"

"No sir, I mean, only a little, from the head . . . the ears, I think."

"Gregory, will you please take pity on us," said Sorensen, making no effort to hide a yawn. He flicked his lit cigarette into the snow.

"The regulations don't say anything about pity," Gregory snapped, looking around again. Wilson was angrily slamming his tripod into position; Thomas was cursing quietly to himself because the powdered plaster in his bag had spilled, and all his instruments were covered with it.

"Well, let's get our jobs done, men," Gregory went on, "prints, measurements, everything, and the more the better; when you finish here go down to the mortuary, but we'd better keep the rope up until later on. Doctor, there may still be something for you . . . wait a minute," he said, turning to the constable. "Where's your commanding officer?"

"In town, sir."

"Well then. Let's go see him."

Gregory unbuttoned his coat; it was getting warm. The constable shifted uncertainly from one foot to the other.

"Do you want me to come along, sir?"

"All right."

Sorensen followed them, fanning himself with his hat. The sun had come up in earnest now, and in its warmth the snow was quickly disappearing from the branches, which now appeared black and wet against the deep blue of the sky. As they walked, Gregory counted the number of paces from the wreck to the point where the cemetery lane joined the road: there were 160. The lane, and the cemetery at its end, lay in the shadows between two hills. It was cool here, and the snow was still wet and heavy; because of the hills nothing could be seen of the town except its smoke. The mortuary itself, a whitewashed little shed, was enclosed by thick underbrush in the rear; there were two small windows on the northern side, and a half-opened door in one wall. Carelessly slapped together with a few odd pieces of wood, the door had a simple latch but no lock. There were footprints all around the area, and just in front of the doorstep they saw a flat canvas-covered shape.

"Is that the body?"

"Yes, Lieutenant."

"Has anyone touched it, or is that the way it was found?"

"Exactly the same, sir. No one touched it. The C.O. took a look at it when he got here with the doctor, but no one touched it."

"What about the canvas?"

"The C.O. told us to cover it."

"Tell me, could anyone have gotten to it while you were on the road?"

"No sir, impossible, the road is closed off."

"On this side. But what about from Hackey?"

"We have a man on guard down there too, but you can't see him from here because of the hill."

"What about the fields?"

"It might be possible," the policeman agreed, "but in that case he'd have to get across the water."

"Water? What water?"

"There's a stream on the other side of the road."

Gregory still hadn't gone near the canvas. Moving carefully to the side, he looked for Williams's footprints. He found a few on the narrow, well-trodden pathway encircling the nearest gravestones; they continued around the long shed, then went back into the shrubbery. Some big footprints like the ones he had seen on the road were clearly impressed in the snow at the spot where the constable had abandoned his post, suggesting that he had lost his way in the dark.

Watch in hand, Gregory timed himself while making a complete circuit around the shed: four minutes. "At night, during the snow storm, it might have been twice as much," he thought, "and maybe two minutes more, give or take, for the fog." Venturing deeper into the thick shrubbery, Gregory found himself walking down a slope. Suddenly, the snow slid out from under him. Grabbing some hazelwood branches he managed to stop himself just before he fell into the stream. The area in which he regained his footing was the lowest point in the syncline in which the cemetery was situated. Even close up it was hard to see the stream because of the high snow drifts along its banks. Here and there he noted the water fretting steadily at the eroded roots of nearby shrubs; embedded in the soft loam at the bottom of the stream he could see stone fragments, some of them similiar in size and shape to paving blocks. Turning around, Gregory had a better view than before of the mortuary's rear wall, but only of the windowless upper portion which loomed over the bushes a few yards away. He took a good look; then, pushing the resilient hazel branches out of his way, began to climb back.

"Where can I find the local stonemason?" he asked the constable. The officer understood immediately.

"He lives near the road, a little way past the bridge. The first house over there, it's a kind of yellowish color. He only does stone work in the summertime; winters he takes on carpentry to make a little extra."

"How does he get his stones over here? By the road?"

"He brings them in on the road when the water is low, but when it's high enough, which only happens once in a while, he floats them over from the station by raft. He enjoys doing that kind of thing."

"Once he gets them here, where does he work on them—over there near the stream?"

"Sometimes, but not always. He works in a lot of different places."

"If you follow the stream from here, does it lead up to the station?"

"Yes, but you can't really go that way because the whole area is tangled with underbrush right up to the edge of the water."

Gregory walked over to the side wall of the mortuary. One of the windows was open—in fact, it was broken, and a jagged piece of the glass pane was half-buried in the snow just beneath it. He peeked inside, but it was so dark that he couldn't see anything.

"Did anyone go inside?"

"Only the C.O., sir."

"Not the doctor?"

"No, the doctor didn't go in."

"What's his name?"

"Adams, sir. We didn't know when the ambulance from London would get here. The one from Hackey got here first, and Dr. Adams came along with it. He happened to be on night duty when the call came in."

"Is that so?" said Gregory, but he was only half-listening to the constable, his attention attracted by a small, light-colored bit of wood shaving stuck to the frame of the broken window and by the deep though not very clear impression of a bare foot in the snow next to the wall. He bent down to get a better look. The snow was all churned up, as if something very heavy had been dragged through it. Here and there he could make out some flat-bottomed oblong depressions; they looked as if they had been made by pressing a large-sized loaf of bread into the snow. Noticing something yellowish in one of them, Gregory bent over still more and picked up a few more curled shavings. Twisting his head around, he looked at the second window for a moment. It was closed and painted over with whitewash. Then, stepping backward a little, he knelt on one knee to brush some of the snow aside, stood up again, and with his eyes followed the course of the strange signs. He took a deep breath. Standing erect, with his hands in his pockets, he glanced at the white space between the bushes, the mortuary, and the first gravestone. The deep, misshapen prints began under the broken window, looped around in an arc to the door, then zigzagged right and left as if a drunk had been pushing a heavy bag. Sorensen stood off to the side, watching all this without much interest.

"Why isn't there a padlock on the door?" Gregory asked the constable. "Was there one before?"

"There was, Lieutenant, but it broke. The gravedigger was supposed to take it to the blacksmith but he forgot, and when he finally remembered it was Sunday, and so on. You know how it is," the constable shrugged.

Gregory, not saying a word, moved closer to the unshapely canvas mound, carefully lifted the edge of the stiff sheet, then pulled the whole thing off and threw it to the side.

This revealed a naked body. It was resting on its side with its arms and legs bent, as if it were kneeling on something invisible or pushing against something. A wide furrow in the snow extended from the lower part of the body to directly under the window. About two paces beyond the body's head was the doorstep. The snow in that space was smooth.

"Why don't you examine him," Gregory suggested, getting up again. The blood rushed to his face. "Who is he?"

he asked the constable, who was in the process of pulling his cap down over his eyes to protect them from the sun.

"Hansel, sir. John Hansel. He owned a small dyeing plant near here."

Gregory watched while Sorensen, wearing a pair of rubber gloves he had taken out of an ordinary briefcase, felt the corpse's legs and hands, drew back the eyelids, and examined the spinal curvature.

"Was he a German?"

"I don't know, sir. Maybe by ancestry, but I never heard anything about it. His parents always lived around here."

"When did he die?"

"Yesterday morning, sir. The doctor said it was a heart attack. He had a heart condition for a long time and wasn't supposed to work anymore but he didn't care. He didn't care about anything after his wife left him for another guy."

"Were there any other bodies in the mortuary?"

Sorensen stood up, brushed his knee with a handkerchief, rubbed an invisible spot off his sleeve, and carefully slipped the rubber gloves back into his briefcase.

"There was one the day before yesterday, sir, but it's already been buried. The funeral was yesterday, at noon."

"So this is the only body that's been here since noon yesterday?"

"That's right sir, only this one."

"Well, Doctor?"

Gregory walked over to Sorensen. They stood together under a willow bush for a moment, but the melting snow on its branches soon began to drip on them.

"What can I tell you?"

Sorensen sounded annoyed.

"Death took place about twenty-four hours ago. The stains on the jaw, as you can see, indicate rigor mortis."

"What about the extremities? Well, speak up—don't you have anything to tell me?"

Both men lowered their voices but they spoke angrily.

"You saw it yourself."

"I'm not a doctor."

"All right—there's no rigor mortis. Not a sign; someone must have interrupted it. Someone interrupted it—let's leave it at that and call it quits."

"It won't come back?"

"Sometimes it does, at least to a certain degree, but not always. Is this very important?"

"Are you sure there was any to begin with?"

"There's always rigor mortis. You should know that. And please don't ask me any more questions because I've already told you all I know."

"Thanks a lot," Gregory said, not bothering to hide his irritation. He walked over to the door. It was still open, but in order to go in he had to step over the body—actually, to jump over it, since the whole area had already been trampled enough and he didn't want to leave any unnecessary footprints. Gregory took hold of the latch from the side and pulled. The door, stuck in the snow, didn't budge. He tugged harder; this time, the door, with a shrill creak, slammed into the wall. It was pitch dark inside, and there was a wide puddle of melted snow on the doorsill. Closing his eyes and waiting patiently until they were accustomed to the darkness, Gregory stood for a moment in the unpleasant cold draft from the walls.

The mortuary was lit slightly by some light from the small northern window—the broken one; the other window, covered with whitewash, was barely translucent. Looking around, Gregory saw a coffin strewn with shavings standing in the center of the beaten earth floor. Leaning against it was a fir and spruce mourning wreath wrapped in a black ribbon with the letters "R.I.P." in gold. The coffin lid stood in a corner against the wall. There were more wood shavings scattered beneath the window; alongside the other wall Gregory saw a pickaxe, a shovel, and several coils of dirty, clay-encrusted rope. There were also a few wooden boards.

Gregory went outside again, closing his eyes for a second in the painful brightness. The constable was covering the corpse with the canvas, trying very hard not to touch it.

"You had the duty until three this morning, right?" asked Gregory, walking over to him.

"That's right, sir." The constable straightened up.

"Where was the body?"

"When I was on duty, sir? In the coffin."

"How do you know? Did you check it?"

"Yes sir."

"How, by opening the door?"

"No sir, but I shined my flashlight through the window."

"Was the windowpane broken?"

"No."

"What about the coffin?"

"I don't understand, sir."

"Was the coffin open?"

"Yes sir."

"What position was the corpse in?"

"The usual one, sir."

"Why wasn't it dressed?"

The constable livened up a little.

"The funeral was supposed to be today, sir. About the clothing—it's a long story, it is. When Hansel's wife walked out on him—that was two years ago—his sister moved in. She's a pretty difficult woman, hard to get along with. Well, he died in the middle of breakfast and she didn't want to give up the suit he was wearing because it was too new. She was supposed to give an old suit to the undertaker, but when he came to pick up the body she told him she'd decided to take an even older suit and dye it black. The undertaker didn't want to make another trip, so he took the body the way it was. She was supposed to bring the suit this morning—"

"Gregory, I want to go back to London. You don't need me here anymore," Sorensen interrupted. "Let me take the car. You can get another one at the station house."

"We'll talk about that in a minute," Gregory snapped. Sorensen was beginning to get on his nerves. A moment later, though, he added, "I'll try to work something out for you." Gregory was staring at the wrinkled canvas. Though he'd only seen the corpse for a few moments, he remembered it vividly. The dead man was a little under sixty years old. He had tired, work-stained palms. His head was almost bald, and there was a gray stubble covering his neck and cheeks. Most distinctly etched in Gregory's memory, however, was the expression of surprise in the half-closed, clouded eyes. It was beginning to get warmer, and Gregory wanted to throw off his coat. He tried impatiently to calculate how long it would be before the sun reached the areas that were still in the shade. It was absolutely necessary to get casts of all the footprints and other markings before the snow melted.

He was about to send the constable up the road when he saw his crew approaching. Gregory walked over to meet them.

"It's about time. Now listen, the snow is beginning to melt so don't waste any time. Thomas, I'm particularly interested in the prints between the window and the door, but the snow is wet, so be careful or everything will fall apart! I'm going into town now. When you finish with the prints, measure everything that looks important, and get the distance from here to the water—there's a stream over there behind the bushes. Take a few pictures of the whole area and search the bank of the stream. I may have missed something."

"Don't worry about it, Gregory," said Wilson. His equipment, slung over his shoulder in a flat bag, kept slapping him on the hip as he walked, making him limp slightly. "And don't forget to send the car to pick us up," he added casually.

"Of course."

Gregory walked back toward the road, completely forgetting about Sorensen. Turning around for a moment, he saw the doctor following him. The ropes blocking off the scene of the accident had already been taken down, and two men in a wrecker were pulling the Bentley out of the ditch alongside the road. His car was standing next to the bridge, turned in the direction of London. Without a word, Gregory slid into the front seat next to Calls. The doctor, noting that the car's motor was already turning over, speeded up his pace. A moment later they drove past the policeman from the highway patrol and headed back toward Pickering.

The police station was located in a two-story building on the market square. With a constable to show him the way, Gregory went upstairs and passed through a long corridor lined with doors. Through the window at one end he could see the roofs of the one-story houses on the other side of the square.

The district commander rose to greet him. He was a long-headed, red-haired man, with a reddish mark from his hatband about halfway down his forehead. His cap lay on the desk beside him.

Smiling nervously, not showing any signs of friendliness or good humor, the commander rubbed his hands together.

"Well, let's get to work," Gregory sighed, settling into a chair. "Do you know how Williams is? Can I speak to him?"

The commander shook his head.

"It's out of the question. He has a skull fracture. I phoned the hospital at Hackey just a minute or two ago.

87

They say he's still unconscious, and according to the doctors it'll be a long time before he comes to—if he ever does."

"I see. Tell me, you know your own men, is Williams a good policeman? How long has he been on the force? In fact, tell me everything you know about him."

Gregory spoke somewhat distractedly. In his mind he was back at the mortuary, still looking at the prints in the snow.

"Williams? What can I tell you? He's been with me for four years. Before that he was up north. He served in the army, was wounded, got a medal. He got married after he came here and has two children. Nothing special to distinguish him. He likes to go fishing. He's even-tempered, reasonably intelligent. No major offenses on his record."

"What about minor ones?"

"Well . . . maybe he was a little too . . . easygoing. But in a good-hearted way, you know what I mean. He had a tendency to interpret the regulations independently. Of course in a town like this everyone knows everybody else . . . but it never involved anything important. He didn't write enough tickets . . . that kind of thing. He was quiet, maybe even too quiet, I would say . . . uh, I mean he is," the commander corrected himself with a wince.

"Did he believe in ghosts?" Gregory asked very seriously. The commander looked at him.

"In ghosts?" he repeated involuntarily. He seemed confused. "In ghosts? No . . . I don't think so. I don't know, really. Are you suggesting that he . . ." He didn't finish. Both men were silent for a moment.

"Have you any idea what he was running away from?" Gregory asked quietly, leaning forward and looking the commander straight in the eye. The commander didn't answer. He lowered his head slightly, then raised it.

"I haven't the slightest idea, but . . ."

"But?"

The commander studied Gregory's face. At last, as if alienated by it, he shrugged his shoulders.

"All right. In that case we'll stick to the facts. Do you have Williams's pistol?"

"I do."

"And?"

"He was holding it in his hand," the commander said in a quiet voice.

"Go on. Did he fire it?"

"No. The safety was still on. But . . . there was a cartridge in the chamber."

"Loaded? What of it? Don't tell me your men go on patrol with their guns unloaded?"

"Why not? This is a quiet town. There's always time to load. . . ."

"How do you think Williams managed to get from the place where the car hit him to where the ambulance crew picked him up?"

A surprised expression came over the commander's face.

"He wasn't able to go anywhere after the accident, Lieutenant. Smithers, the man who hit Williams, says he moved him. . . ."

"I see. Well, that certainly simplifies things. Let's say that . . . well, it simplifies things," said Gregory. "Do you have Smithers here?"

"Yes."

"I'd like to question him, if that's all right with you."

"Of course."

The commander opened the door and said a few words to someone, then walked over to the window. A minute or so later a slim, good-looking young man in tight-fitting flannel trousers and a bulky-knit sweater walked in. He had narrow hips and the face of a B-movie leading man; pausing in the doorway he glanced nervously at Gregory, who was leaning back in his chair and watching him with a searching look. After a moment Gregory spoke.

"I'm down from the Yard to handle the investigation here. You may be able to help me clear up a few things."

Smithers nodded his head slowly.

"I . . . actually, I've already told the whole story . . . I'm innocent—believe me, it wasn't my fault."

"If you're innocent, you have nothing to worry about. Now then, the charge against you is causing an accident and endangering human life. The law does not require you to provide any information that could form the basis of a criminal indictment against you. Are you willing to answer my questions?"

"Yes, yes . . . of course . . . I . . . don't have anything to hide," stammered the young man, obviously quite frightened by the formal statement Gregory had just recited to him. "Please sir," he continued, "there wasn't a thing I could do . . . he just threw himself in front of the car. It was nighttime and there was all that fog—by the time I saw him it was too late. I was driving very slowly, I swear it, and I did everything I could to avoid hitting him. . . . I even smashed the car up because of him. But it was all his fault, and to make matters worse it isn't even my car. . . . I don't know what I'm going to do."

"Please, Mr. Smithers," Gregory said. "Tell me the whole story as accurately as you can. How fast were you going?"

"No more than thirty miles an hour, so help me God. Because of all the fog, and it was snowing too. I could hardly see. In fact, I couldn't even put my headlights on because that would have made it worse."

"You mean you were driving with your lights off?"

"No, never in the world. My foglights were on, but even so I couldn't see more than ten or fifteen feet ahead. All of a sudden he was right in front of the car—believe me, please, he must have been blind, or crazy—he ran straight at me and simply threw himself under the car."

"Did he have anything in his hands?"

"Excuse me, sir?"

"I asked if he was holding anything in his hand?"

"I didn't notice at the time. Afterward, when I picked him up, I saw that he was holding a pistol, but during the accident I didn't notice a thing. I just stepped on the brake as hard as I could, the car went into a spin and turned completely around, and I smashed into the tree. I got pretty badly cut," he said, pointing to his forehead.

There was a thick red line of clotted blood running across Smithers's forehead and disappearing beneath his hair.

"I didn't even feel it at the time, I was so scared," he continued. "For a minute I thought I had managed to miss him. I mean, I really did miss him and I still don't know how he got hit when I skidded—maybe it was the bumper. He was lying in the snow. I began rubbing him with snow—I wasn't even thinking about myself, although the blood was running down into my eyes. He was out cold and my first thought was to get him to the hospital, but I couldn't get my car started—something was knocked out of kilter, I don't know what—so I ran up the road and made a phone call from the first house."

"Why did you carry him to the side of the road instead of to the car?"

"Well . . ." the young man hesitated, "because . . . because, uh, they say you should always keep an unconscious person flat on his back and there wasn't enough room in the car. And I thought that if I left him in the middle of the road someone else might run over him. . . ."

"Good. What time did all this happen?"

"A little after five. Maybe ten or fifteen minutes after."

"Did you see anyone on the road when you were going to the telephone?"

"No, not a soul."

"What about earlier, when you were driving? Did you see anyone? Pedestrians? Cars?"

"Pedestrians, no. Cars? No, no cars either; I did pass two trucks, but that was while I was still on the expressway."

"Where were you coming from?"

"London."

The room was silent. Smithers walked over to Gregory.

"Inspector, please . . . am I free to go now? And what about the car?"

"Don't worry about the car," said the commander, who was still standing near the window. "If you want, my men can take it to a garage for you, we'll tow it over ourselves. There's a good one not far from here—we'll take the car over and you can get it repaired."

"Thank you. That'll be perfect. Only I'll have to wire home for some money. May . . . May I go now?"

Gregory and the commander glanced at each other and came to a silent understanding. With an affirmative nod, Gregory turned to Smithers. "Please leave your name and address," he said. "An address where we can reach you if necessary."

Smithers turned to leave, then stood for a moment with his hand on the doorknob.

"Uh . . . the constable . . . how is he?" he asked quietly.

"He may come out of it. We don't know yet," said the commander. Smithers opened his mouth as if to speak, then walked out of the room without another word.

Overcome by an incomprehensible feeling of fatigue, Gregory turned to the desk and rested his head in his hands. More than anything he would have liked to sit quietly for a while, not talking, not thinking.

"What was he running away from?" he suddenly blurted out, surprising even himself. "What the hell was he running away from?"

"You mean 'who,' don't you?" said the commander, taking his seat behind the desk again.

"No. If he had trouble with a human being he would have used his gun, wouldn't he? As sure as two and two make four he would have, don't you agree?"

"Did you look over those prints yourself?" asked the commander. He was busily trying to push the strap of his cap through its buckle. Gregory took a good look at him. The commander of the Pickering police station had wrinkled cheeks, bloodshot eyes, crow's feet; there were already a few gray strands scattered through his red hair.

"What was the situation when you got there?" Gregory parried the commander's question with a question of his own. The commander, with great concentration, was working on his buckle.

"The man on duty in the station was Parrings. That kid, Smithers, called at about half past five. Parrings woke me up right away—I live in the house next door. I told him to contact the Yard, then started out as fast as I could."

"Was it still dark when you got there?"

"It was brightening up a little, but there was a thick fog."

"Was it snowing?"

"No, not anymore."

The commander put his cap down; the dangling chin strap slapped against the desk.

"The doctor was busy with Williams when I got there. Williams is a big man, so I helped the doctor and the driver lift him into the ambulance. Meanwhile, two men from the highway patrol arrived on the scene. I posted them on the road to keep the accident area clear, and then I went down to the cemetery by myself."

"Did you have a flashlight?"

"No, but I took Hardley's—he's the highway patrol sergeant. I found the body lying on the ground just outside the door, its head facing the door sill. The door was open."

"What position was the body in?"

"Arms and legs bent. I think they call it a geniculate position."

"Where did you get the canvas?"

"I found it inside the mortuary."

"You mean you went inside?"

"Yes. Sideways. You know, I jumped over the door sill. Maybe I missed something in the dark, but the only prints I saw around the mortuary were Williams's, and I thought there might still be someone inside—" He stopped abruptly.

"You mean you thought the perpetrator was still there?"

"Right."

The decisive tone of the answer took Gregory by surprise.

"What made you think so?"

"Something moved when I shined my light inside. . . ."

Hunched over and twisted around in his chair, Gregory studied the commander's face. They were no more than two feet apart, maybe a little less. Clearly in no hurry to continue, the commander raised his eyes. A vague smile crossed his lips, as if he was a little ashamed of what he was going to say.

"It was a cat. . . ."

He tapped a finger against the surface of his desk and added, "I have him here."

"Where?"

Gregory took a quick look around the room, but the commander shook his head. "Here. . . ."

He opened a drawer, revealing a small package wrapped in newspaper. After a moment's hesitation he put it on the desk. Gregory carefully pulled back the folded edge of the paper and saw a skinny white kitten with a black tuft at the end of its tail. Its fur was wet and tangled, its paws unnaturally stiff, and the narrow, dull pupil of one eye was staring at him.

"He's dead?" Gregory turned to the commander in bewilderment.

"He was still alive when I first entered the mortuary."

"Huh?"

Gregory's cry was involuntary.

"When did he die?"

"He was yowling in agony. When I picked him up he was already beginning to get stiff."

"Where did you find him?"

"Near the coffin. He was sitting . . . on the wreath."

Gregory closed his eyes for a moment, then opened them and looked at the cat, covered him with the newspaper again, and placed the package on the windowsill.

"I'll have to take this for an autopsy or something," he muttered, wiping his forehead.

"What made you bring the cat back to the station?" he continued.

"The prints. You didn't see any paw prints, did you?"

"No."

"Because there were none," the commander explained. "All I had with me was a flashlight, but I looked around very carefully. The cat didn't leave any prints in the snow."

"In that case how did he get into the mortuary?"

"I don't know. He must have been there before it started snowing."

"When was that?"

"Sometime after eleven. Maybe a little later. I can get the exact time for you."

"Good, but how did he get in? Maybe he was there the whole time."

"He wasn't there earlier in the evening. Constable Sticks had the duty till three o'clock. From eleven till three. The cat must have slipped in sometime during his tour."

"Did Sticks . . . did he open the door?"

"Yes, when he first came on duty. He's very conscientious—wanted to make sure everything was in order when he began his tour. I checked this with him myself."

"I see. So that's when the cat slipped in."

"I suppose so."

Thomas and Wilson came into the room.

"All ready, Lieutenant. Everything's finished. Calls is driving the doctor to the train station but he'll be back in a few minutes. Are we going now?"

"Yes. Put this in the trunk of the car. Sorensen is going to get a little extra work," said Gregory, not without a certain amount of malice. He shook hands with the commander.

"Thank you very much for all your help. If it's at all possible I'd like to have Williams transferred to a hospital in London. Meanwhile, please get in touch with me if anything else comes up, all right?"

They went downstairs. Gregory glanced at his watch and was surprised to see that it was already past noon. He began to feel hungry.

"Let's have something to eat," he said to the others. There was a small restaurant nearby, a little place with tables and a lunch counter. Calls drove past just as they were sitting down. Wilson ran out to get him, and, after parking outside the restaurant, the sergeant came in and joined them. The four men ate in silence. Wiping his dark, slightly too elegant mustache, the photographer ordered some beer for himself and turned to Gregory.

"Can I buy you a drink, Lieutenant?"

"No thank you," said Gregory.

The sergeant joined in declining the offer. "I'm driving," he explained.

By the time they finished eating it was nearly two o'clock. The snow had melted, except for some grayish ice sparkling on the rooftops, and there were puddles of dirty slush all over the street. Gregory suddenly felt like driving. The men piled into the car, Calls next to him in the front seat, the other two in the back, and he pulled away from the curb, kicking up a fountain of muddy water. As he accelerated, Gregory peeked out of the corner of his eye to see whether the sergeant thought he was driving too fast, but Calls was staring out the window with a glazed, sleepy expression on his face. Gregory drove well, although, in his own opinion, a little too stiffly; this had always been a matter of some concern to him because he very much wanted to achieve the indifferent nonchalance, the automatic composure that marked the experienced driver, and he was able to maintain this pose only as long as he could keep his mind on something else. The tires hissed shrilly as he drove up the street and within a few minutes the windshield was covered with thousands of dark exclamation points. Past Wimbledon the traffic got heavier. Gregory was tempted to turn on the siren to clear the way, but since they weren't really on an emergency call his scruples wouldn't permit him to satisfy this desire. They reached London about an hour later. Wilson and Thomas had work to do in the lab. Gregory asked the sergeant to drop him off at home. The two of them were alone in the car, and when they reached his house Gregory didn't get out. Instead, he offered Calls a cigarette, lit one himself, and then spoke:

"Did you see . . . out there?"

Calls nodded his head slowly, then rolled his window down.

"Sergeant, we've known each other for a long time. Tell

me what you really think about all this. Is there anything you would run away from, even if you had a loaded pistol in your hand?"

Raising his eyebrows slightly, Calls glanced quickly at Gregory; then, with great deliberateness, flicked his ash. It looked as if he wasn't going to say anything, but suddenly he blurted out:

"A tank."

"Come on, you know what I'm talking about."

The sergeant took a deep drag on his cigarette.

"I looked around pretty good myself, sir. The way I see it, this Williams is circling the place the way he's supposed to; somewhere around five, or a little after, he sees something he don't like too much. He don't clear out right away, though. That's important. He stands his ground . . . draws his pistol, only he don't have time to release the safety."

"Couldn't he have drawn his pistol after he started running?" Gregory asked. His eyes sparkled as he studied the sergeant's face. Calls smiled unexpectedly.

"You know yourself it can't be done. These holsters of ours are pretty tight. You saw those footprints, didn't you? This guy took off like a bat out of hell. A man who's running like that can't wrestle with a holster flap. He had to get it open first. Even in the worst fog you can see a pair of headlights at thirty feet, especially if they're shining right in your face. But Williams didn't see them, he didn't see nothing. Whatever it was, it really got him."

"Who would an armed constable run away from?" Gregory repeated, a blank expression on his face. He didn't expect an answer, and he didn't get one.

4.

"Well?" said Sheppard. Gregory handed him the written report.

"This is a complete summary, sir."

Sheppard opened the folder and began reading:

"9:40 A.M. J. Hansel dies at breakfast of heart attack. Dr. Adams certifies death.

"2:00 P.M. Undertaker arrives. Hansel's sister doesn't want to give clothing. Undertaker puts naked body in coffin, takes it to mortuary.

"5:00 P.M. Constable Atkins begins tour at mortuary. Body in open coffin. Door held shut by piece of lath stuck through latch.

"11:00 P.M. Constable Sticks begins tour. Checks mortuary by opening door. No changes. Begins to snow. N.B. Cat may have slipped into mortuary around this time while Sticks not looking.

"3:00 A.M. Williams relieves Sticks. Doesn't open door, shines flashlight through window in presence of Sticks, who ascertains nothing is changed, then returns to town.

"5:25-5:35 A.M. Smithers telephones Pickering police station, reports running over policeman.

"5:50-6:00 A.M. Ambulance from Hackey arrives on scene with Dr. Adams. Pickering police commander arrives on scene. Williams, still unconscious, taken to hospital. He has fractured skull and three broken ribs. Bentley sedan smashed into tree about 183 yards from mortuary; either trunk or rear bumper hit Williams. Commander proceeds to mortuary, ascertains that door is half-open; finds corpse, contractile, lying on side, about three feet in front of door;

99

one window of mortuary broken, pane smashed from inside, pieces of glass embedded in snow. Commander finds cat inside mortuary. Takes it with him. Cat goes into convulsions, dies on way to town.

"Prints discovered around mortuary:

"1. Footprints of Constable Williams, corresponding to impression of his boots; in circular path around mortuary, then veer away from mortuary, head toward broken window, then toward road, ending up at scene of accident.

"2. Footprints of Pickering police commander. Difficult to distinguish since they follow directly on Williams's prints, obliterating part of outline left by instep.

"3. One very clear print of bare foot, identified as left foot of dead man, found just outside broken window of mortuary; facing toward wall, toes turned slightly inward; print very deep, as if impressed by substantial weight.

"4. Prints leading from window around corner of building to door; may have been made by someone crawling on all fours or creeping. Marked depression of prints suggests indentations made by pressure of knees. Prints well preserved in two places where snow very compressed: features indicate prints made by bare skin.

"5. Paw prints of cat, corresponding in size and shape to paws of dead cat. Found about 30 yards from mortuary in direction of stream in deep snow among bushes; prints disappear near mortuary as if cat climbed up on bush.

"6. Human footprints found on soft bottom of stream (deepest part, near mortuary, about 16 inches), at distances of 139, 133, and 123 feet respectively from mortuary. Prints probably formed by boots but washed out, not very clear, providing insufficient basis for identification; time of formation impossible to determine; according to lab, possibly two to six days ago.

"Observation (a). Wood shavings found in indentations

mentioned in item 4 and under window were identical to shavings in coffin.

"Observation (b). Indentations mentioned in item 4 led to place where body was found but not as far as door (distance measured in feet).

"Observation (c). Distance from path where Constable Williams's footprints were found to bank of stream, measured in straight line at shortest point, was 42 feet; area concerned is covered by dense thicket consisting mainly of hazel bushes. Measuring from behind mortuary, where slope is fairly gradual, to stream bank (which is some 19 inches higher than bottom of stream), vertical differential is about 5 feet. All along bottom of stream and throughout thicket, even at densest point, we found stone fragments, ranging in size from smaller than a potato to larger than a human head; these were apparently left in area at various times by mason who makes grave markers for cemetery.

"Condition of corpse: In addition to what is already noted in detailed report of postmortem examination (attached), N.B. Observation of extremities revealed no signs of rigor mortis although its presence was ascertained by undertaker the day before yesterday. Since reversal could not have been effected normally in such a short time (ordinarily rigor mortis does not set in until 15 16 hours after death), someone must have impeded its development."

Sheppard looked up at Gregory.

"Do you know anything about rigor mortis, Lieutenant?"

"Yes, of course, sir. I made a special point of checking all this with the experts. Rigor mortis can be interrupted by the application of force, after which it either does not return or returns in a much weaker form."

Sheppard put the report down.

"Have you arrived at any conclusions?" he asked.

"You mean about how the crime was committed?"

"What else?"

"The perpetrator must have sneaked into the mortuary even before Atkins went on duty," said Gregory. "He hid there, either in a corner, behind the coffin, or in among the boards and ropes piled along the wall in the back. Around five o'clock he took the body out of the coffin, moved it to the window, and pushed out the windowpane. Williams heard the noise of the breaking glass, came over to take a look, and drew his pistol when he saw the broken glass and the open window. Meanwhile, the perpetrator had started pushing the corpse through the window. To Williams it looked as if the corpse was moving by itself. He panicked and started running. After Williams disappeared, the perpetrator climbed through the window and started dragging the corpse toward the door; apparently he then heard or saw something which frightened him, so he dropped the body and ran."

"Which way?"

"It was around five-thirty, give or take a few minutes, just a little before daybreak. He followed the footpath to the edge of the thicket, made his way through the thicket without leaving footprints by stepping from stone to stone and along the heavier branches, then lowered himself into the stream from an overhanging branch and, keeping to the water and stepping on stones wherever possible, headed in the direction of the railroad station."

"Is that the whole thing?" Sheppard asked.

"No," said Gregory. "There's a variant. The perpetrator arrived on the scene by way of the stream at around four or a little after. Watching from the stream he waited until Williams was on the other side of the mortuary, then climbed up the slope through the thicket. Since the storm didn't stop for another hour and a half, any footprints were soon covered by fresh snow. The perpetrator followed Williams along the footpath at a safe distance, then unhooked the door of the mortuary, went inside, and closed the door again. From then on he proceeded as in the first variant: took the body out of the coffin, pushed out the pane, attracted Williams's attention, shoved the corpse through the window, and, when Williams ran away, dragged the corpse to the door, refastened the latch, and returned to the stream. But instead of going to the station, he followed the stream to the point where it passes under the expressway. His car was waiting there and he drove away."

"Did you find anything on the expressway?"

"A few tire tracks, but nothing definite. Don't forget that everything I've told you is still only conjectural—we can't be sure of anything until we talk to Williams. If he remembers the door being closed, but without the lath in the latch, we'll accept the second variant."

"How is Williams doing?"

"Still unconscious. The doctors say his case will be settled in two or three more days, one way or the other."

"Yes . . ." said Sheppard. "You'll have to come up with a better reconstruction, otherwise we have only one alternative: '. . . and for fear of Him the keepers did shake. . .' "

Gregory's eyes wandered from the Chief Inspector's face to his hands, which were resting motionlessly on the desk.

"Do you really think so?" he asked slowly.

"Gregory, I really wish you would think of me as your ally rather than your adversary. Try to put yourself in my place for a moment. Is my request really so funny?" Sheppard asked quietly, noticing that the lieutenant had begun to smile.

"No. I just remembered something. I also . . . anyway, it doesn't really matter. If I were you, I'd still think the same way I do now. You can't go through the wall if there's no door."

"Good. Let's go over the first variant. The perpetrator,

you said, sneaked into the mortuary sometime before the first constable went on duty at eleven o'clock. Here's a floor plan of the mortuary. Show me where he could have hidden."

"Here in the corner behind the big coffin, or in the opposite corner behind the boards."

"Did you try any of these places yourself?"

"Well, more or less. . . . You can get behind the big coffin, but it wouldn't be much good as a hiding place if anyone shined a light in from the side. That's why I say it must have been the boards. None of the guards made a systematic search of the mortuary; at best they only looked in through the door."

"Good. Now, the corpse was stiff, so to get it through the window the perpetrator had to change its position, right?"

"Yes. And in the dark too. Then he had to break the window and drop the body out."

"How did he manage to get the corpse's footprint into the snow next to the wall?"

"I don't think that would have been too hard for him."

"You're wrong, Gregory, it would have been extremely difficult. He had to do it without attracting Williams's attention, but Williams had already been drawn to the scene by the sound of the breaking glass. From the perpetrator's point of view, this must have been a damned critical moment. We can be certain that Williams wouldn't have run away if he'd seen the perpetrator. Someone moving a corpse around wouldn't have frightened him—after all, he knew very well that he'd been assigned to the mortuary to watch out for just that kind of thing. Maybe he would have used his pistol, maybe he would have tried to apprehend him without weapons, but he certainly wouldn't have just run away. Do you see what I mean?"

Gregory was looking the Chief Inspector straight in the eye. Finally, with a brief gesture, he nodded his assent.

104

Sheppard continued.

"Now, if the corpse had fallen into the snow and the perpetrator was nowhere near the body—let's say he was squatting behind the window and couldn't be seen from outside—even then Williams wouldn't have run away. He would have drawn his pistol and waited to see what happened next. He might have decided not to go inside, but he would have kept his eye on the door and the window. Whatever he did, though, he wouldn't have run away. Do you go along with this also?"

Gregory nodded his head again, staring at the floor plan on the desk.

"We have the same problem with the second variant. None of it is very probable except the part about how the perpetrator got inside, since it doesn't depend on him hiding behind the boards as suggested in variant one. The snow could certainly have covered his footprints as you said. Let's continue. From this point on, according to both variants, the incident took the same course. After Williams ran away, the perpetrator left the mortuary, pulled the corpse over to the door, and then escaped by way of the bushes and the stream. But what was the purpose of dragging the body through the snow—and in point of fact he didn't drag it at all, as we both know very well, but did something quite peculiar: he made it look as if a naked man had been crawling around on his hands and knees. Right?"

"Yes."

"Why would he do something like that?"

"The situation is much worse than after our first conversation . . ." Gregory said, his tone quite different from what it had been until now, as if he had an unexpected secret to tell. "It was easy enough to get inside the mortuary if all the factors were taken into account. He could easily have followed the constable—it was a dark, windy night and it was snowing—once inside the mortuary he could have waited, let's say, forty-five minutes or an hour, in order to let the snow cover his footprints. But as for the rest . . . I couldn't help thinking for a while that he wanted to produce the very effect you mentioned; in fact, once I accepted the idea of someone trying to set up a situation that would force the police to believe there had been some kind of resurrection, I thought our investigation had come to the end of the line. But now we can't even consider that theory anymore. The perpetrator moved the corpse but then left it at the scene. Maybe something frightened him away, but why did he leave the corpse in the snow? One look at the corpse is enough to prove that it didn't come back to life. He must have known that, but even so he moved it, and in a way that made it appear as if it had moved itself. None of it makes any sense—not in criminal terms and not in terms of insanity."

"Maybe he did get frightened away, as you said just a minute ago. Maybe he heard the approaching car."

"Yes, he could even have seen it, but—"

"Seen it? How?"

"When you turn off the expressway for Pickering, your headlights—the expressway is on somewhat higher ground, you see—shine into the cemetery and light up the roof of the mortuary. I checked it last night."

"Gregory, that's important! If the perpetrator was frightened by the lights of a car, and if that's what caused him to abandon the corpse, we may have our explanation. Furthermore, it would be his first blunder, his first failure to carry out a well-planned act. He panicked and dropped the corpse. Maybe he thought the police were coming. That should be the basis of your reconstruction. . . . At any rate, it's an out!"

"Yes, it's an out," Gregory admitted, "but . . . I can't take a chance on it. We're dealing with a man who studies weather reports and plans his actions in accordance with a complicated mathematical formula. He would certainly have known that the lights of a car coming around the turn from the expressway would light up the whole area for a moment, including the cemetery."

"You seem to have a great deal of respect for him."

"I do. And I absolutely refuse to believe that anything frightened him away. An armed constable standing right there didn't scare him. Would he have been afraid of a couple of headlights off in the distance?"

"Things like that happen. The straw that breaks the camel's back . . . Maybe it took him by surprise. Maybe it confused him. You don't think it's possible? You're smiling again? Gregory, you seem to be absolutely fascinated by this person. If you're not careful, you'll end up being . . . a disciple!"

"I suppose that's a possibility," said the lieutenant in a caustic tone of voice. He reached for the report but, discovering that his fingers were trembling, hid his hand under the table. "Maybe you're right . . ." he said after a moment's reflection. "I can't help feeling that everything I found out there was exactly the way he wanted it to be; I don't know—maybe I'm beginning to go crazy. Only . . . Williams wasn't frightened by the corpse but by what was happening to it. Something happened to that body that made him panic. We may find out what it was, but will we ever know why. . . ."

"There's still the matter of the cat," Sheppard mumbled as if talking to himself. Gregory lifted his head.

"Yes. And, to tell the truth, that's a lucky break for me."

"How do you mean that?"

"Right from the beginning this case has been characterized by a fantastic consistency—every incident has certain features in common with all the others—incomprehensible, perhaps, but definitely all following the same pattern. In other words, no matter how it looks, this business isn't chaotic. It has to do with something real, although we haven't the slightest idea of its purpose. Chief Inspector . . . I . . . even though, as you said, I myself . . ."

Uncertain whether he was making himself clear, Gregory began to feel nervous.

"I realize we can't do anything except increase the surveillance. That is, we can't do anything right now, but this case will come to a head once he uses up all his alternatives. . . . He's been relentlessly consistent so far, and one day we'll turn that consistency against him. Sciss will help by telling us where to expect the next incident."

"Sciss?" repeated Sheppard. "I just received a letter from him."

He opened his drawer.

"He says there won't be any more incidents."

"What?" Completely flabbergasted, Gregory stared at Sheppard, who nodded his head quietly.

"According to him, the series is over, either indefinitely or . . . forever."

"Sciss said that? On what basis?"

"His letter says he's working on the documentation now, and would rather not explain anything until he's finished. That's all."

"I see."

Trying hard to regain his composure, Gregory took a deep breath, straightened his lanky torso, and studied his hands for a moment.

"I suppose he knows more than we do. Did he see the results of my investigation?"

"Yes. I turned them over to him at his own request. We certainly were obligated at least to that extent, since he enabled us to pinpoint the places where the incidents would take place. . . ."

"Yes, yes. Of course," Gregory repeated. "This . . . this changes everything. There's nothing else we can do, if . . ."

He stood up.

"Would you like to talk to Sciss?" asked Sheppard.

Gregory made a vague gesture: more than anything, now, he wanted to leave the Yard, to be by himself, to end this conversation as quickly as possible. Sheppard rose from his chair.

"I wish you wouldn't be so impatient," he said in a low voice. "In any case, please don't take offense. So far as that goes, please . . ."

Gregory retreated toward the door. Somewhat disconcerted by the look of expectation on Sheppard's face, he swallowed and said with some effort:

"I'll try, Chief Inspector, but I don't think I'm ready to talk to him yet. I don't know. I still have to . . ."

He left without finishing. In the corridor the lights had already been turned on for the evening. The day seemed to be so indescribably long, Gregory thought; he felt as if the incident yesterday had taken place weeks before. He rode down in the elevator; then, surprising himself by his impulsiveness, he got off on the second floor, and headed for the laboratories, his steps muffled by a deep carpet. Here and there old-fashioned brass doorknobs glowed dimly, polished by the touch of thousands of hands. Gregory walked slowly, his mind a blank. Through an open door he saw some spectrographs mounted on stands; near them, a man in a white lab coat doing something with a bunsen burner. A few more steps and he reached another open door. Inside, covered from head to toe with white powder and looking more like a baker than a technician, he found Thomas. The room, jammed with long, even rows of strange-looking twisted blocks of hardened plaster, looked like the studio of an abstract sculptor. Thomas was bending over a long table with a wooden mallet in his hand, apparently about to release his latest creation from its mold. A basin of soft plaster stood on the floor beside him. Gregory leaned against the door and watched him for a few moments.

"Oh, hello," Thomas said, looking up. "I'm just about finished. Do you want to take it with you?" He began shifting the casts around, eying them with professional satisfaction.

"A nice clean job," he muttered to himself. Gregory nodded, picked up a white, surprisingly light block of plaster which was standing near the edge of the table, and, glancing at its bottom, saw the impression of a naked foot with big, thin, widely spaced toes. Along the edges the plaster had risen slightly to form a mushroom-like rim.

"No thank you, not now," said Gregory, putting the cast down and hurriedly walking out of the room. Thomas watched in surprise, then began to remove his splattered rubber apron. Gregory, already in the corridor, stopped and asked over his shoulder:

"Is the doctor in?"

"He was a few minutes ago, but he may have left already. I don't know."

Gregory walked to the end of the corridor. Without knocking, he opened the door and went into the medical examiner's lab. The window was shaded, but a small lamp next to a nearby microscope stand provided some light. Here and there, he could see racks of test tubes, beakers and other instruments, and some glistening bottles of colored liquid. There wasn't a sign of Sorensen, but Dr. King, his young assistant, was sitting at his desk, writing.

"Good evening. Is Sorensen around?" Gregory asked; without waiting for an answer he began to bombard King with questions.

"Do you know anything about the cat? Did Sorensen examine—"

"Cat? Oh, the cat!"

King stood up.

"I ought to know—I did the autopsy. Sorensen isn't here. He said he was too busy." King's emphasis suggested that he was not especially loyal to his boss. "I still have the cat," he continued. "Do you want to take a look?"

He opened a small door in the corner of the room and turned on the ceiling light. The only article of furniture in the narrow cubicle was a dirty wooden table; it was splattered with reagents and rust-colored stains. Gregory glanced in at the reddish sliced-up thing pinned to the table and backed away.

"Why should I look?" he said. "You're the doctor. Tell me what you found."

"Well, in essence . . . mind you, I'm not a veterinarian," King began, straightening up slightly. With a mechanical gesture he touched the row of pens and pencils in the breast pocket of his jacket.

"Yes, yes, I know that, but I wanted the autopsy done right away and there wasn't time to get a vet. Now how about it, Doctor, what did the cat die of?"

"Starvation, cold, exposure. He was such a pathetic, skinny little creature."

"How's that?"

King, without knowing why, was annoyed by Gregory's astonishment.

"What did you expect? Poison? Believe me, there was none. I made all the usual tests, but it was hardly worth the trouble. There was absolutely nothing in the cat's intestines. You look disappointed."

"No, no, you're right, of course. Nothing else?" Gregory asked, staring at some instruments spread out in the sink. Lying next to a pair of forceps was a scalpel; some scraps of fur still adhered to its blade.

"I'm sorry," said Gregory. "Uh, thank you for your trouble, Doctor. Good night."

Gregory turned and walked into the corridor. A few seconds later he was back. Dr. King, busy with his papers again, raised his head.

111

"Excuse me, Doctor . . . was the cat very young?"

"No, not at all. In fact, it was rather old. Don't let the small size fool you—it's a characteristic of the breed."

Though he sensed that he wouldn't get anything more from King, Gregory, resting his hand on the doorknob, continued to ask questions.

"Uh . . . is there any chance that the cat died from something unusual?"

"What do you mean by 'something unusual'?"

"Uh, maybe some kind of rare disease . . . oh, never mind, you already told me the cause of death, I'm just talking nonsense. Excuse me . . ." Noting the derisive expression on King's face, Gregory was genuinely relieved to get back to the corridor. He closed the door and stood next to it. Before long he heard the sound of King whistling.

"Well, maybe I put him in a good mood," he thought, "but I've had it."

Gregory ran down the stairs and into the street. The lights in the building were already on for the night, but outside it was still only early evening. A strong southerly wind was drying the sidewalks. Gregory strolled along whistling, but stopped as soon as he realized he had picked up the tune from King. There was a slender woman walking a few steps in front of him. Gregory noticed a stain of some kind on the back of her coat. No, it was a feather, or maybe a shred of cotton. Catching up with the woman to tell her about it, Gregory opened his mouth and began to raise his hand to his hat in greeting; inexplicably he returned his hand to his pocket and quickened his pace. It was only a little while later, when he had given some thought to the incident, that he realized why he hadn't said anything. The woman had a pointed nose.

"I shouldn't worry about such stupid things!" he told himself angrily.

Entering a subway station, Gregory boarded the first northbound train. He leaned against the side of the car, glancing through a newspaper and mechanically peeking over it from time to time to check the names of the stations rushing past outside the windows. He got off at Wooden Hills. The train pulled away noisily and sped into the tunnel. Gregory stepped into an unoccupied telephone booth and opened the directory. Carefully sliding his finger along the column of names, he found what he was looking for: "Sciss, Harvey, Ph.D., M.A. Bridgewater 876-951." He picked up the receiver and dialed the number carefully, closing the booth door in anticipation. No more than a minute later he heard the even buzz of the ringing signal, then a short clicking and a woman's voice:

"Hello?"

"Is Dr. Sciss in?"

"No he isn't. Who's calling?"

"Gregory, of Scotland Yard."

The woman hesitated for a moment, as if uncertain what to do. Gregory could hear the sound of her breathing.

"The Doctor will be back in fifteen minutes," she said at last, a note of reluctance clearly discernible in her voice.

"In fifteen minutes?" he repeated.

"Probably. Shall I tell him you called?"

"No, thanks anyway. Maybe I . . ."

Gregory hung up without finishing and stared glumly at his hand, which was pressed against the telephone book. Noticing the flickering lights of an approaching train, he left the booth without further thought, glanced quickly at the illuminated platform sign to find out the destination of the waiting train, and got into the last car.

During the twenty-minute trip to Bridgewater, Gregory kept thinking about the woman who had answered Sciss's phone. He knew Sciss wasn't married. Could it have been his mother? No, the voice was too young. Housekeeper? He tried desperately to remember its sound, flat yet melodious at the same time, as if it were a matter of extreme importance, but he was well aware that he was only trying to keep from worrying about what to say to Sciss. Their conversation, he was afraid, might eliminate his only remaining lead.

In Sciss's neighborhood the subway line ran outdoors on an elevated structure. Gregory descended from the station and, with the noise of passing trains rattling overhead, walked along a broad avenue lined by stores. Sciss lived nearby on a dimly lit, deserted street; a bright green sign advertising a peep show glowed in the ground-floor window of the house next to his.

It was hard to see much of Sciss's building in the darkness. Gregory noticed some masses of concrete protruding over the sidewalk from the upper stories; they could have been ledges or balconies. The building's entrance lobby was completely dark, except for some light reflected from a neon sign across the street; the stairway was dark also. Gregory pushed an illuminated button for the self-service elevator and rode upstairs. Sciss would probably use that damned logic of his to make fun of him, he brooded; Sciss never lost a chance to demonstrate his superiority to everyone else, and he'd probably leave Sciss's apartment feeling defeated and convinced of his own stupidity.

The hallway on Sciss's floor was almost totally dark, but a thin crack of light revealed that his door was open slightly. "I should ring the doorbell anyway," Gregory said to himself, gently pressing his finger against the button. The door swung open without a sound. Gregory walked in; the air in the apartment was warm, dusty, and very dry, and there was a peculiar odor, a cool subterranean odor of decay, something like the stench of a tomb, he thought. The odor was so out of place that it startled him. Wrinkling his nose slightly, Gregory stood in the foyer for a few moments to get accustomed to the darkness, then began feeling his way toward a line of light visible some distance in front of him.

Before long he came upon a slightly opened door which led into a larger room. Near the wall, and partly blocked

114

from his view by the open door of a closet, a desk lamp stood on the floor. A huge triangular shadow was moving on the ceiling, looking something like a gigantic bird flapping its wings one at a time.

At the other end of the foyer, behind him, Gregory heard the hissing whistle of a gas burner and the dripping of a water faucet. Except for these two sounds, the apartment was absolutely silent—no, not quite, for he could hear someone breathing laboriously.

The room was large and square. At one end a dark curtain partly covered a window. The walls were lined with books. Gregory stepped inside and spotted Sciss; the scientist was sitting on the floor next to the desk, surrounded by bulging folders which he was apparently trying to put into some kind of order by the light of the desk lamp beside him. The room felt even warmer than the foyer, the air exuded the dryness characteristic of apartments with central heating; the unpleasant musty odor became even more discernible.

The situation was peculiar, and Gregory stood at the door not knowing what to do. While he waited, the minutes dragged on . . . and on. Sciss, sitting with his back to Gregory, continued to work on his folders, which apparently had been removed from the open drawers of his desk. He carefully brushed the dust off some, blew it off others with a disgusted snort, waving them back and forth. Somewhere behind Gregory, probably in the kitchen, the gas hissed continually. He thought he could hear someone moving around, probably the woman he had spoken to on the phone. Gregory took another step into the room; the floor creaked, but Sciss didn't notice. Finally, yielding to an admittedly senseless impulse, Gregory knocked loudly on the open door of the closet.

"What's that?" Sciss said, turning his triangular head with its disheveled hair in the detective's direction.

"Good evening and . . . please excuse me," said Gregory a little too loudly. "I don't know if you remember me, I'm Gregory of Scotland Yard. We met each other at Headquarters, at Chief Inspector Sheppard's. . . . Your outer door was open, and—"

"Yes, I remember. What can I do for you?"

Sciss rose to his feet, accidentally kicking over the nearest pile of folders, and sat down on his desk, wiping his fingers with a handkerchief.

"I'm in charge of the investigation in this . . . case," Gregory said, finding it difficult to choose the right words. "Chief Inspector Sheppard told me about your letter. You said you don't foresee the possibility of further . . . further incidents. That's what I came over to ask you about. . . ."

"Indeed. But I said in my letter that I can't provide an explanation right now. I'm working alone and I don't know if . . ."

He cut himself off in mid-sentence, revealing an uncertainty that was not at all typical of him. Shoving his hands in his pockets and taking long, stiff steps, Sciss walked across the room, passing in front of the detective, who was still standing in the same spot. Near the window, he swung around, sat down on the radiator with his arms clasping his knees, and stared into the light of the lamp on the floor.

Sciss remained silent for several minutes; then, without any preliminaries, began speaking. "Anyway, maybe even that's not so important. There's been a change in my plans . . . quite a radical change."

Gregory stood with his coat on, listening, but realizing at the same time that Sciss was thinking out loud, hardly aware of his presence.

"I went to the doctor. I haven't been feeling well for a long time, and there has been a significant drop in my productivity. On the basis of averages determined from the ages of my parents, I calculated that I had thirty-five years more. I forgot to consider the effect of intensive intellectual

116

work on my blood circulation. It seems that I have . . . a lot less time. It puts a new complexion on things. I still don't know if—"

Sciss stood up so abruptly and with such decisiveness that it looked as if he intended to terminate the visit by abandoning Gregory and leaving the room. Such behavior from Sciss wouldn't have surprised Gregory at all. He didn't doubt the truth of what Sciss had told him, but he hardly knew what to make of it. The peaceful, lifeless composure in Sciss's voice was completely at odds with his impulsive movements: he jumped to his feet, took a few steps, sat down here and there like an irritated, exhausted insect—there was something poignant about him, and it was reflected in his tired, almost despairing tone of voice. In the end, Sciss didn't leave the room after all. Instead, he sat down on a couch along the wall opposite the window. Just over his birdlike head, casting a slight shadow on the ragged gray hair around his temples, there hung a picture, a print of Klee's "The Madwoman."

"I had made plans for the next twenty years. The ten years after that I was holding in reserve. Now I have to change everything, I have to go over all my plans and drop everything secondary, everything that isn't original research. What isn't secondary—when you have to carry a bottle of nitroglycerin around! I don't want to leave any of my work unfinished."

Gregory remained silent.

"I don't know whether I can continue on this case. In the long run the problem is trivial—the hypothesis needs a few minor adjustments, that's all, but I don't like that kind of work, it doesn't interest me. Furthermore, a complete analysis of all the relevant statistical data would take weeks maybe even months if the right computers aren't available."

"Our people—" Gregory began.

"Your people would be useless," Sciss interrupted. "This

isn't a criminal investigation, it's a scientific study." He stood up and continued, "What do you want—an explanation? You'll get it, don't worry."

He glanced at his watch for a moment.

"And I was about to take a rest," he said. "This case has nothing at all in common with criminology. No offense of any kind was committed, no more than when someone is killed by a meteor."

"You mean that the operative causes are . . . forces of nature," Gregory asked, immediately regretting it because he had resolved to keep his mouth shut and let Sciss do all the talking.

"I don't have time for discussions, so please don't interrupt me. Can you define those 'forces of nature' you mention so glibly? I can't. The problem in this case is strictly methodological. Its aspects from the criminal point of view don't interest me at all, they never did."

Without interrupting himself, Sciss went over to the wall, turned on the ceiling light, and glanced at the lieutenant. A smile appeared on his thin lips.

"Please look over here." He pointed toward the open closet. Gregory moved closer. There was a map of England hanging on the door, its surface covered with what looked like a fine red rash, but the blood-red speckling wasn't uniform in intensity: in some places it was denser; here and there towns were completely encircled; the lightest areas were on the right-hand side of the map, along the Channel coast.

"Since this isn't really a problem for you or your department, you'll probably find my explanation useless, but I assure you it's the only answer," Sciss said, smiling faintly but coldly. "Do you recognize the lightest area over here?"

"Yes. That's the area of Norfolk where the bodies were stolen."

"Wrong. This map shows the distribution of deaths from

118

cancer in England for the past nineteen years. The region with the lowest death rate—that is, less than thirty percent, using an average based on a half-century—falls within the boundaries of the area in which the corpses disappeared. In other words, there is an inverse proportion; I have formulated an equation to express it, but I won't go into that now because you wouldn't understand it." Sciss's almost imperceptible smile was beginning to take on an abusive quality.

"It is your primary duty to respect the facts," Sciss continued. "I, my dear sir, went beyond the facts. Some corpses disappeared. How? The evidence suggests they walked away by themselves. Of course, you, as a policeman, want to know if anyone helped them. The answer is yes: they were helped by whatever causes snail shells to be dextrorotatory. But one in every ten million snail shells is sinistrorsal. This is a fact that can be verified statistically. I was assigned to determine the connection between one phenomenon and other phenomena. That's all that science ever does, and all that it ever will do—until the end. Resurrection? By no means. Don't be ridiculous. The term is used much too loosely. I'm not claiming that the corpses came back to life, with their hearts beating, their brains thinking, the coagulated blood in their veins flowing again. The changes which take place in a dead body are not reversible in that sense. What other sense is there, you ask—the corpses moved around, changed their positions in space. I agree, but the things you're talking about are nothing but facts—I have explanations!"

Sciss moved closer to the map and raised his arm. No longer smiling, he spoke quickly and energetically, his high-pitched voice taking on a triumphant note.

"A phenomenon is subject to analysis only if the structure of its events, as in this case, conforms to a regular pattern. Science progresses by discovering the connection between one phenomenon and other phenomena, and this is exactly what I succeeded in doing. If I were to ask why a rock falls when dropped, you would reply that it is due to the action of gravity. Yet if I asked what gravity is, there would be no answer. But even though we don't know what gravity is, we can determine its regular pattern of action. People become accustomed to rocks always falling. Any phenomenon which continues to exist within everyday comprehension, even if incomprehensible in itself, ends up being commonplace. For example, if human or animal corpses usually got up and walked around, if that was the norm, the police wouldn't be interested in the incidents in Norfolk. I was assigned to determine the cause of this seemingly abnormal series of phenomena, and, its uniqueness notwithstanding, to connect it with some other series of phenomena that was already familiar, documented, and of such long standing that its occurrences no longer shock the public or arouse the curiosity of the police. Death by cancer is a perfect example of this kind of phenomenon. I examined parish registries from the whole Norfolk region as well as hospital death records for the past fifty years. Of course I encountered a certain amount of difficulty. During the early part of this fifty-year period doctors were not able to differentiate cancer, or to treat it as a separate disease as they do nowadays. However, to the extent that it was possible, I collected the facts regarding the number of cancer-related deaths, translated them into statistics, and transferred them to this map. You can see the results."

Sciss turned off the light and went back to his desk, and as he did so Gregory finally discovered the source of the unpleasant odor: it was emanating from the corner just beyond the closet, where he could see some long, low boxes crammed with moldy, stained, old books.

"To make a long story short, Mr. Gregory, mortality due to cancer follows a regular cycle and is in turn governed by it. Around the end of the nineteenth century we begin to see an irregular but steady increase in incidences of cancer, and nowadays, as a result, more people than ever contract cancer and die from cancer. Norfolk and its surrounding region, however, constitutes an enclave with a relatively low cancer mortality. In other words, the rate of death from cancer has remained more or less the same for the past thirty years, although it has continued to increase in adjacent regions. When the difference between the mortality rates of this enclave and the adjacent localities exceeded a certain level, corpses began to disappear. The center, that is, the place where the first disappearance occurred, is not the geometric, spatial center of the enclave, but the place in which cancer mortality reached the lowest level. The phenomenon spread from that point in a definite pattern: it moved rapidly because of such factors as temperature, etc. As you should remember, I've already explained that. In the last incident, the phenomenon reached the boundaries of the enclave. The formula which I have derived from the statistics on cancer deaths excludes the possibility of any corpse disappearances outside the enclave. It was on this basis that I wrote to Sheppard."

Sciss fell silent, turned around, and picked up the lamp. He held it in his hand for a moment, as if uncertain what to do with it, then placed it on his desk.

"You made up your mind on the basis of this?" Gregory whispered, warning himself to proceed cautiously.

"No. There was more."

Sciss folded his arms across his chest.

"In the earlier incidents, the corpses disappeared, so to speak, 'permanently'; that is, they were moved for an unknown distance in an unknown direction. In the last incident, however, there was comparatively little displacement of the corpse. Why? Because the last incident occurred very close to the boundary of the enclave. This helped me to define the coefficient of my formula with great precision, inasmuch as the rate of cancer mortality increases by an arithmetic rather than a geometric progression as we trace its passage from the enclave into the adjacent regions."

The room was silent. Gregory could hear the far-off hissing of the gas burner.

"All right," he said at last. "In your opinion, then, what caused the disappearances? The movements, if you prefer."

Sciss smiled faintly, looking at the detective with an amused expression.

"I beg your pardon," he said, "but I've already answered your questions. You're acting like a child who is shown Maxwell's theorem and a diagram of a radio receiver and then asks, 'How does this box talk?' It has never occurred to you or your Chief to institute an investigation against whatever causes people to contract cancer, has it? Similarly, at least as far as I know, you've never made inquiries about the perpetrator of Asiatic flu."

Gregory clenched his teeth, warning himself not to respond to Sciss's sarcasm.

"All right," he said. "The way you see things you're right. Since it's only a simple case of resurrection, rather than a matter of corpses moving, standing, and walking after death, you consider everything to be perfectly clearcut and understandable and therefore not worth any further investigation."

"Do you think I'm an idiot?" Sciss said, sitting down on the radiator again. His voice was suprisingly gentle. "Obviously there's a good deal here for biochemists, physiologists, and biologists to look into, but there's nothing for the police. Futhermore, the study of something like this could go on and on without any definitive results, even after fifty years—just like the study of cancer. Only my field—statistics—can give immediate results. The same applies in the study of cancer. So far as this case is concerned, there will probably be quite a few conflicting theories in time, and I imagine that the ones the public finds most appealing will help to build up the circulation of the more sensational newspapers. The phenomenon will be connected with flying saucers, with astrology, with God only knows what. But all that is none of my business."

"What about the dead animals we found at the scene of the disappearances?" Gregory asked, pretending not to have heard the note of anger that was beginning to appear in Sciss's voice.

"That interests you? Yes, of course . . ." Sciss said. Suddenly calm again, he clasped his knees with his thin, twisted arms.

"I didn't analyze that particular point mathematically, but the simplest and most fundamental explanation would be to regard the animal as a *vehiculum,* that is to say, as the carrier or medium which conveys the movement factor to the corpse. This factor is specific to a particular biological *agens;* it is similar in nature to whatever causes cancer, and in certain circumstances, we must assume, the 'something' that produces cancer is transmuted into our factor, that is, it employs small domestic animals as a means of moving from one place to another. Rats, to cite a well-known example, played the same role in bubonic plague."

"Is it some kind of bactéria?" Gregory asked. He was leaning against the open door of the closet, studying Sciss's shadow on the floor in front of him but listening carefully.

"I didn't say that. I don't know. I don't know a thing. The theory is full of holes. *Hypotheses non fingo.* I won't stand for it. It isn't my job to formulate hypotheses. I can't afford to worry about the problem, I haven't got the time."

"If it's not a bacteria, but, as you say, a biological factor, maybe it's a microbe," Gregory said. "An intelligent mi crobe, in fact a very intelligent microbe, a microbe with the ability to think ahead the way a human being does."

"I get the impression that you're looking for a way to

make a profit on this story—what are you planning, a magazine article about intelligent microbes?" Sciss's voice shook with anger. Gregory, as if he hadn't heard, walked slowly toward Sciss, very slowly, speaking more and more distinctly, yet faster and faster, as if he were being consumed by the fire of a brilliant idea.

"This factor," Gregory said, "suddenly turns up in the middle of the area that has the low death rate. It carries out all its activities with as much foresight as a conscious being, except that at the beginning it's still inexperienced. It doesn't know, for instance, that most people would consider a naked corpse a little—let's say—peculiar, and that carrying one around can get a bit complicated. Then the factor learns that nudity is considered improper dress, even on dead people. The next time he moves a body he makes a point of providing suitable clothing—and how does he do it?—by tearing down a curtain with his bare teeth! Later on he learns to read; how else is he going to study the weather forecasts? Then this brilliant intelligence of his fogs up when he gets too close to the boundary of the low cancer mortality region. He can only manage to set some stiffened limbs in motion—poorly coordinated motion at that—and run them through some graveyard gymnastics: standing the body up, making it peer through the window of the mortuary, and so forth."

"You seem to know exactly what happened. Were you there?" Sciss asked, not showing his face.

"No, I wasn't there, but I know what can frighten an English constable. Dancing corpses. Evidently just as he was losing consciousness he remembered Holbein and the pranks skeletons used to play in the Middle Ages."

"Who?"

The scientist's voice was almost unrecognizable.

"What did you say?" Gregory asked in surprise. "What's this 'who?' We're talking about a statistically documented biological factor. I'm just repeating what you told me."

Gregory drew so close to Sciss that he was almost able to touch his knee. The scientist stood up, thrusting his pale, motionless face directly in front of the detective's. Gregory could see his pupils contracting. The two men stood that way for a few moments, then Gregory stepped backward and began laughing. The laugh was feigned, but it sounded almost spontaneous and its naturalness would have fooled anyone. Sciss stared at him for a moment, then his face began to quiver spasmodically and he started to laugh also. An instant later the room fell into silence. Sciss returned to his desk, sat down in the armchair behind it and, leaning backward, drummed his fingers on his leg for a moment.

"You think I did it, don't you?" he said. Gregory had not expected such directness. Uncertain how to reply, he stood quietly, tall and clumsy, desperately trying to decide how to handle things now that their encounter had taken this new course.

"A few moments ago," Sciss continued, "I thought you considered me an idiot. I can see now, though, that you think I'm insane. And so . . . I am threatened with arrest or with detention for psychiatric observation. Considering my state of health, I must say that both eventualities come at a bad moment; in addition I really can't afford to waste the time. I was wrong to let Sheppard talk me into cooperating, but it's too late now. What can I do to convince you that your theory is wrong?"

"Did you go to the doctor today?" Gregory asked in a quiet voice, drawing closer to the desk.

"Yes. I saw Dr. Vaugham. His office hours are from four to six. I made an appointment with him by telephone last week."

"The results of his examination . . . are they medically confidential?"

"I'll phone him and ask him to tell you everything he told me. Is there anything else?"

"Is that your car parked in the courtyard downstairs?"

125

"There are always several cars in the courtyard so I don't know which one you're talking about. I have a gray Chrysler."

"I'd like—" Gregory began. He was interrupted by the telephone. Sciss bent over and picked up the receiver.

"Sciss speaking," he said. The drone of a loud voice could be heard in response.

"What?" said Sciss. Then, a little louder: "Where? Where?"

For the next few moments he listened without saying a word. Gregory moved closer to the desk. He looked at his watch. It was almost nine.

"Good. Yes . . ." Sciss said at last. Just before hanging up he added: "Yes, yes, Gregory is here, yes, I'll tell him." He slammed the receiver into its cradle, stood up, and walked over to the map inside the open closet door. Gregory followed him.

"One of the missing bodies has been found," Sciss said, his voice so low that he appeared to be thinking about something else. He peered nearsightedly at the map and, taking a pen from his pocket, made a small mark near the edge of the enclave.

"In Beverly Court, at the bottom of a water tank. It was discovered when the tank was drained. The body of a male."

"Who telephoned?" asked Gregory.

"What? Uh, I don't know. I didn't ask. He told me his name but I wasn't paying attention. It was someone from Scotland Yard. Sergeant something-or-other. Yes, it fits. They'll all start turning up now . . . in sequence, like shells fired from a gun, although . . ."

He became silent. Standing slightly to Sciss's side, Gregory watched him through slitted eyes, listening intently to the rhythm of his breathing.

"You think they'll come back . . . all of them?" he said

126

at last. Sciss raised his eyes to Gregory and quickly straightened up. His face was flushed, his breathing even louder than before.

"I don't know. It's possible, it's even probable. If they do, the whole series will be concluded . . . and everything else with it! Maybe I figured it out too late. Suitable camera equipment with infrared film would have provided photographs explicit enough to protect me from this . . . this fooling around."

"Does Beverly Court fit into your pattern? What I mean is, does its location go along with your theory?" Gregory asked somewhat perfunctorily.

"The question is poorly phrased," Sciss replied. "I have no way of determining where the bodies will be found; that is, where they will ultimately stop moving. The only thing I can calculate is the amount of time that elapses between a disappearance and the cessation of the phenomenon, and this I can do only approximately. In my estimate, the bodies which disappeared first will be found last. You should be able to understand why. At the beginning, for some reason, the factor conveyed the greatest amount of motor energy to the corpses; by the time it reached the boundary of the region it was only able to transmit a minimal charge, barely sufficient for a series of uncoordinated body movements. You probably think I'm raving. Or lying, perhaps. It's all the same thing in the end. Now leave me alone, will you? I still have a lot to do." Sciss pointed to one of the boxes of moldy books. Gregory nodded his head.

"I'm going. Just one question first. Did you go to the doctor by car?"

"No. I went by subway and I came home the same way. I have a question too: what do you intend to do with me? I only ask because I want to be able to work as long as possible without interference. Is that understood?"

Gregory buttoned his coat, which was beginning to hang

on his shoulders like a lead weight. Taking a deep breath, and again inhaling the faint musty odor, he answered:

"What do I intend to do? Nothing, for the time being. Let me remind you that I haven't expressed any suspicions or made any charges—not even one word!"

With his head bent, Gregory walked into the foyer. In the dimness he caught a glimpse of a woman's face, a pale blot which disappeared almost instantly; he heard the sound of a door slamming. He found his way out of the apartment, checked the time again on the luminous face of his watch, and went downstairs. In the lobby, instead of heading for the street, he turned in the opposite direction and went into the courtyard toward a long, gray automobile. He circled it slowly but couldn't see very much in the faint light from the windows of the surrounding buildings. The car was locked, completely dark, except where reflections of the apartment house lights danced rhythmically on its shiny fender in time with Gregory's movements. He touched the hood: it was cool. That didn't mean anything, though. It was a little harder to reach the radiator. He had to bend down and stretch his hand through a wide chrome-enclosed gap that looked like the thicklipped mouth of a sea monster. Hearing a slight noise, Gregory winced and straightened up. He saw Sciss at the second-floor window. Now he wouldn't have to continue his examination of the car, Gregory thought; Sciss's behavior confirmed his suspicions. At the same time, though, he felt a bit uncomfortable, as if he had been caught doing something underhanded, and this feeling became stronger when, observing Sciss more closely, he realized that the scientist wasn't watching him at all. After standing next to the open window for a few moments, Sciss sat down awkwardly on the window sill, drawing his knees up and wearily resting his head in his hands. This gesture was so imcompatible with Gregory's image of Sciss that he stepped back to get a better look, and as he did so he stumbled over a piece of metal, crushing it underfoot with a piercing noise. Sciss looked down into the courtyard. Gregory stood absolutely still, flushed with embarrassment and anger, uncertain what to do next. He didn't know for sure if he'd been seen, but Sciss continued looking downward, and although Gregory couldn't make out his eyes or face, he could feel his disdainful gaze.

Completely crestfallen and not daring to continue with his examination of the car, Gregory walked away, his head lowered and his back hunched.

Before he reached the subway he had regained his composure, at least to the extent that he was able to go over the ridiculous incident in the courtyard—ridiculous, he thought, to have allowed it to upset him. Gregory was almost certain he had seen Sciss's car in downtown London that afternoon. He hadn't noticed the driver, but it was the same car all right—there was a distinctive dent in the rear bumper. At the time Gregory hadn't paid much attention to the car. The chance incident did not begin to take on significance until later, when Sciss claimed to have gone to the doctor by subway rather than by car. The discovery that Sciss was lying wasn't too important in itself, but, Gregory felt, if he had known earlier in the evening he would have been somewhat less scrupulous and cautious in his behavior toward the scientist; furthermore, it would have counteracted the feeling of compassion which had overcome him during the unfortunate visit. Gregory still didn't know anything definite, however, and whatever certainty he could derive from his afternoon observation of the car was based on a wretched "maybe" and thus didn't count for much. His only satisfaction came from knowing he had discovered an inconsistency in what Sciss had told him. Sciss had gotten rid of him by claiming he had work to do, but instead of working he had done nothing but lounge around the window. Gregory remembered Sciss's state during the visit: his

129

listless body, the inclination of his head, his exhausted leaning against the window frame. But if Sciss's fatigue was the ultimate cause of their disagreement, Gregory had not taken advantage of it, ultimately, because of a stupid gallantry which prevented him from exploiting his opponent's moment of weakness and made him leave the apartment perhaps no more than a minute before the decisive words were uttered.

Drawn into a labyrinth of possibilities by these thoughts, Gregory, impotently angry, wanted only to return home and study the facts in his thick notebook.

It was almost eleven o'clock when he got off the subway. Just before turning the corner to the Fenshawe house, he passed a blind beggar stitting in a niche in the wall of a building, a bald, ugly mongrel at his feet. The beggar had a harmonica, but blew into it only when someone was approaching, using it as a signal without any pretence of making music. It was impossible to determine his age, his clothing providing more clues than his face, which was hidden by a nondescript beard. Returning home late at night or leaving before daybreak, Gregory always met the same beggar in the same place, like an inescapable pang of conscience. The beggar was as much a part of the neighborhood landscape as the big bay windows of the house in front of which he sat, and although Gregory was a policeman and the police regulations prohibited begging, it never occurred to him that he was tacitly consenting to his presence and thus was a party to a misdemeanor.

Gregory never gave much thought to the beggar—in fact, the old man's clothing was so filthy that the very sight of him aroused disgust—but the beggar, nonetheless, must have stirred something in his memory; indeed, awakened feelings deep in his subconscious, for Gregory always quickened his pace almost involuntarily when passing him. Gregory never gave anything to beggars: it had nothing to do with his profession, nor was he an unkind person; perhaps the cause was some indefinable shame. This evening, though, having already passed the old man's post, spotting the dog crouching at his side (sometimes he felt sorry for the dog), Gregory surprised himself by turning and walking over to the dark wall, taking some money out of his pocket as he did so. There followed one of those insignificant little incidents that one never mentions to others and remembers ever afterward with an indescribable feeling of distress. Assuming the beggar would reach out to accept it, Gregory extended the hand with the money into the vague darkness of the niche. When he did, however, his fingers brushed against those disgusting, filthy rags. The same thing happened again and again; the beggar grotesquely lifted his harmonica to his lips and began blowing. Overcome by a feeling of revulsion, and unable to find a pocket in the torn material covering the huddled body, Gregory blindly threw the money down and backed away. Something clattered at his feet—in the weak light of the street lamp he saw that it was his own coin rolling after him. Gregory picked it up and impulsively pressed it into the darkened indentation in the wall. He was answered by a hoarse, stifled groan. Desperate now, Gregory rushed home, taking such long strides that he seemed to be running. He didn't recover from his agitation until he had reached the front of his house. Then, seeing a light in the window of his room, he ran upstairs without any of his usual caution, reaching the door slightly out of breath. He stood in front of the door for a moment, listening carefully. Not a sound. Glancing at his watch again—it was 11:15—he opened the door. Sitting and reading at Gregory's desk, just in front of the glass doors opening on the terrace, was Sheppard. He raised his head from the book:

"Good evening, Lieutenant," said the Chief Inspector. "It's about time you got here."

5.

Gregory was so taken aback that he couldn't answer for a moment. He stood in the doorway without removing his hat, a foolish expression on his face. Sheppard smiled faintly.

"Why don't you close the door?" he said at last, when the tongue-tied scene had dragged on a little too long. Pulling himself together, Gregory hung up his coat and shook hands with the Chief Inspector, watching him expectantly.

"I came over to find out what you accomplished at Sciss's place," said Sheppard, sitting down at the desk again and resting his elbow on the book he had been reading. The Chief Inspector spoke calmly, as usual; detecting a note of irony in the word *accomplished,* however, Gregory adopted a tone of naive sincerity in his reply.

"But Chief Inspector," he babbled, "all you had to do was tell me you were interested, and I would have phoned you. That doesn't mean I'm not glad to see you, of course, but why did you bother to go out of your way—" Sheppard, however, made no effort to carry his end; it was clear that he saw through Gregory's act and, with a slight gesture, he cut off the flow of words.

"Let's not play cat and mouse, Lieutenant," he said. "It was very clever of you to figure out that I'm not here to listen to one of your stories. You made a blunder tonight, a very big blunder, when you set up that telephone call. Yes, the phone call to Sciss while you were at his house. You had Gregson phone him about an allegedly recovered body so you could observe his reaction. And before you start explaining, let me venture a guess that you didn't accomplish anything with your little trick. I'm right, aren't I?"

The Chief Inspector's last words were angry. Rubbing his cold hands gloomily, Gregory straddled a chair and muttered:

"Yes."

All his garrulousness seemed to have disappeared. Sheppard pushed a box of Player's toward him and, taking a cigarette himself, continued:

"It was a cheap trick par excellence, Gregory, a classic. You didn't learn a thing, or almost nothing. Sciss, on the other hand, knows that you suspect him or will know it by tomorrow, which comes to the same thing; furthermore, he'll also know that you set up the call to trap him. All the same, assuming you're right—that he is either the perpetrator or an accomplice—then you did him a favor by warning him. And so far as that goes, didn't it occur to you that someone as cautious as the perpetrator seems to be, now that he's gotten such a clear-cut warning, will become ten times more cautious?"

Gregory was silent, chewing almost furiously on his fingernails. Sheppard, the calmness in his voice contradicted only by a deep furrow between his eyebrows, went on:

"Whether or not you tell me the details of your plan of operations is your business, because I always try, as much as possible, to respect the autonomy of the officers conducting investigations for me. But it was downright stupidity not to tell me you suspected Sciss! I could have told you quite a few things about him, not as his boss but as someone who has known him for a long time. I suppose you've already eliminated any doubts you have about my innocence in this case?"

Gregory's cheeks turned red.

"You're right, sir," he said, raising his eyes to the Chief

Inspector. "I acted like an idiot. And I have no excuse at all, except that I absolutely refuse to believe in miracles, and nothing is going to make me, even if I go crazy."

"We all have to be doubting Thomases in this case—it's one of the unfortunate requirements of our profession," said Sheppard, cheerful now that Gregory's embarrassment had provided him with a degree of honorable satisfaction. "In any event, I didn't come over to reprimand you but to offer you some help. Let's get back on the subject. How did it go at Sciss's?"

Emotionally uplifted by this unexpected reprieve, Gregory described his visit to Sciss with great gusto, not omitting even those points which put him in a bad light. Around the middle of the story, when he came to the part about how he and Sciss burst into laughter after a tense silence, Gregory heard a muffled sound from behind the wall. He bristled internally.

Mr. Fenshawe was beginning the nightly acoustical mystery.

Gregory began to speak faster and with more glibness. He became flushed with excitement. Sooner or later the Chief Inspector was going to notice the noises, whatever they were, and then he'd be mixed up in this weird business too. Barely able to think coherently or to imagine what might happen next, Gregory listened as the sounds increased in volume, reacting to Mr. Fenshawe's wall with the same obstinacy he would have exhibited in response to the pain caused by the extraction of a tooth. A series of rattling noises was followed by several soft, moist slaps. Raising his voice, Gregory talked faster and still faster with a kind of strained eloquence, hoping the Chief Inspector would be too distracted to notice the noises. And for this same reason, undoubtedly, he didn't stop talking when he reached the end of the story. Instead, overwhelmed by the desire to drown out Mr. Fenshawe, he undertook something which in other circumstances he would have kept to himself: an elaborate analysis of Sciss's "statistical hypothesis."

"I don't know where he got the cancer story," Gregory said, "but I'm sure there really is an enclave with a low death rate. Of course we ought to make a large-scale comparative study of all Europe to find out if there are any other enclaves like the one in Norfolk. If there are, it would knock the bottom out of his theory. I didn't discuss any of this with him, but he's right about one thing: if his theory is valid, this really isn't a job for us. The idea of the police checking out a scientific hypothesis is too funny for words. Still, so far as the theory's long-range consequences are concerned, Sciss was very clever. Instead of trying to confuse me with fantastic possibilities, he made it into a joke. But there aren't any alternatives. I've been giving this theory a lot of thought. This is what I've come up with. I'll give you the more conservative variant first. The assumption is that we're facing some kind of peculiar mutation that causes cancer; an unknown virus of some kind, let's say. The reasoning goes this way: cancer manifests itself in an organism as chaos; the organism itself, representing order as it is found in the life processes of a living body, is the antithesis of chaos. Under certain conditions, this chaos factor—that is, cancer, or, more accurately, the cancer virus—is mutated, but it remains alive, vegetating in whatever medium is its host. When the victim stops being sick, the virus goes on living in his corpse. Ultimately, it undergoes such a complete transformation that it develops entirely new powers; it changes from a factor that causes chaos to one that tries to create a new kind of order—a kind of posthumous order. In other words, for a specific period of time it fights against the chaos represented by death and the decomposition of the body that follows death. To do this, the new factor tries to restore the life process in an organism whose body is al-

136

ready dead. When a dead body begins moving around, it's a sign that this process is going on. The moving corpses, in other words, are produced by a weird symbiotic relationship between the living—that is, the mutated virus—and the dead—the corpse itself. Since human reason isn't capable of understanding everything, it's irrelevant whether or not this explanation makes sense. It is important, however, that the order factor is able to initiate highly sophisticated, well-coordinated movements: an ordinary virus wouldn't be able to make a corpse get up, find some clothing for it, and then sneak it away so skillfully that we can't find it again."

Gregory paused, seemingly awaiting Sheppard's reaction; in reality the wall had distracted him with a gentle, repetitive pattering—it sounded as if a light rain was falling on Mr. Fenshawe's side.

"A cancer virus is within the realm of probability," Gregory continued, "but since the improbable can't be explained in terms of the probable, we may have to find an improbable explanation for this case. That's why Sciss mentioned flying saucers, although he tried to be casual about it. He wanted me to know that we may have to look for the answer in outer space. The second variant involves cosmic forces. We're faced with something along the lines of a 'first contact' between Earth and a race of people from the stars. It goes this way: there are beings of some kind out there, intelligent but functioning in a manner completely beyond our comprehension. They want to study human beings at close range, so they send some kind of—information-gathering instruments, let's call them—to Earth, using a method of transportation that we can't understand yet. Maybe the saucers deliver them. The information-collectors are microscopic—invisible for all practical purposes. Once on Earth they ignore living organisms and are directed—programmed would be a better word—only to the dead. Why? First, so they won't hurt anyone—this proves that the star people are humane. Second, ask yourself this. How does a mechanic learn about a machine? He starts it up and watches it in operation. The information-collectors do exactly the same thing. They start up some human corpses, getting everything they want to know in the process. If this variant is correct, there are several good reasons why we can't understand the phenomenon. First of all, the information-collector seems to act rationally; therefore, it isn't a device or tool in our sense of the word. It's probably more comparable to a hunting dog: in other words, some kind of trained bacteria. Second, there's the problem of the connection between the information-collector and cancer. If I was forced to figure out a theoretical basis for linking the second variant with the cancer phenomenon, I'd do it this way: there are just as many cancer viruses in the low-mortality enclave as anywhere else. So if most people in the enclave don't get cancer, it's because they're immune to it. Therefore, human immunity to cancer is inversely proportional to immunity to the something from outer space. This theory explains everything, and we don't have to abandon our statistics. . . ."

Gregory paused. His room, like Mr. Fenshawe's next door, was silent. During this whole presentation Sheppard had listened quietly, occasionally looking as if Gregory's fervor surprised him more than his ideas.

"Obviously you don't believe any of this. . . ." the Chief Inspector commented.

"Not a bit," Gregory answered in a weak voice. He suddenly felt indifferent to everything. He didn't care whether or not the other side of the wall was quiet. All he wanted, just as when he left Sciss's place, was to be alone. The Chief Inspector continued:

"You've done so much research that you hardly sound like a policeman anymore. Well, I suppose it's a good idea to master the enemy's language. . . . Sciss would probably consider you a good pupil. You still suspect him, don't you? What do you think his motive is?"

"It's not that I suspect him," Gregory answered. "If I did I'd make a formal accusation. Actually, I'm more on the defensive, and my position is quite hopeless. I feel like a cornered rat. I only want to defend myself against the allegedly miraculous character of this case. After all, sir, to develop this kind of theory to its full extent, you have to include everything. Let's say, for example, that there are periodic interventions of factor X separated by long time intervals; that the last drop in cancer mortality took place about two thousand years ago—not in England but in the Near East; that there was a series of alleged resurrections then also—you know, Lazarus, and . . . the other one. . . . If we take this story seriously even for one moment, the ground opens up beneath our feet, our whole civilization turns into jelly, people can appear and disappear, everything is possible, and the police should just take off their uniforms, disperse, and disappear . . . and not just the police. We must have a culprit. If this series has really stopped, then it will soon be nothing but past history and we won't have anything to show for it but a couple of plaster casts, a few contradictory stories told by some not too bright mortuary workers and gravediggers—and what kind of investigation can we conduct with that? Finally, the rest of our investigation will probably concentrate on getting the bodies back. You're absolutely right: my trick didn't accomplish anything, the phone call didn't surprise Sciss at all, and yet, wait a minute—"

Gregory leaped from his chair, his eyes blazing.

"Sciss told me something concrete after the phone call. He said he expects the corpses to be recovered, and he claims he can use his formula to figure out exactly where they will reappear, that is, when their energy of movement, as he calls it, will be used up. . . . Now it's up to us to do everything possible to make sure that the reappearances take place in front of witnesses, at least once."

"Just a minute," interrupted Sheppard, who had been trying for some time to get Gregory's attention. The detective, almost running around the room in excitement, seemed for a few moments to have forgotten that the Chief Inspector was there.

"You've set up an either-or proposition: Sciss—or the factor. Now you've practically eliminated the factor, leaving us with nothing but some kind of crude fraud, a gruesome little game being played out in the mortuaries. But what if neither alternative is valid? What if the perpetrator isn't Sciss or the factor? Or what if the perpetrator invented the factor, then injected it into the corpses as an experiment?"

"Do you really believe that?" Gregory screamed, running up to the desk. Panting breathlessly, he stood there, staring at the calm, almost complacent Chief Inspector. "Do you really believe that . . . that . . . nonsense? No one invented anything! A discovery like that would be worth a Nobel Prize! Believe me, the whole world would know about it. That's one reason. And furthermore, Sciss—"

Gregory stopped short. During the acute silence that followed, a slow, measured, creaking sound could be heard, not from behind the wall but in the very room where he was sitting with the Chief Inspector. Gregory had heard this sound a few times before. The incidents had been several weeks apart, but each had occurred while he was lying in his bed in the dark. The first time the creaking had awakened him from a deep sleep. Absolutely certain that someone was approaching him on bare feet, Gregory had switched on the light. There was no one in the room. The second incident had occurred very late—in fact, just before dawn. Gregory, exhausted by a sleepless night of listening to Mr. Fenshawe's acoustical gymnastics, was lying in a state of torpor, neither asleep nor awake. He'd turned on the light again; like the first time, the room was empty. The third time, having convinced himself that the wooden floors in old houses dry unevenly, and that the process can only be heard during the still hours of the night, Gregory ignored the creaking. Now, however, the room was well lit by the lamp on the desk and the furniture, undoubtedly as old as the floor, wasn't making a sound. The parquet near the stove creaked faintly but distinctly. Soon after, somewhat closer to the middle of the room, two more creaks followed in quick succession, one in front of Gregory, the other behind him. After a minute of quiet during which Gregory remained hunched over without moving, a weak sound could be heard from Mr. Fenshawe's room, a kind of giggling— or was it crying?—weak, senile, muffled, perhaps by a quilt—followed by weak coughing. And then it was quiet again.

"And furthermore, Sciss partially contradicted himself. . . ."

Gregory tried to pick up the thread, but the interval had been too long and he couldn't pretend that nothing had happened. He was at his wits' end. Shaking his head a few times as if trying to knock some water out of his ears, he sat down.

"I'm beginning to understand," said Sheppard, leaning back in his chair. There was a serious expression on his face. "You suspect Sciss because you think he has a compulsion to do these things. I suppose you've tried to determine his whereabouts during each of the nights in question. If he has a good alibi for even one of them, your suspicion collapses—unless you accept the idea of an accomplice, a miracle-worker *per procuram*. Well?"

"Is it possible that he didn't notice anything?" flashed through Gregory's mind. "It can't be. Maybe . . . maybe he didn't hear it. Maybe it's old age." He struggled to concentrate. Sheppard's words were still ringing in his ears but he couldn't grasp their meaning.

"Well yes . . . of course . . ." he muttered. Then, regaining control of himself: "Sciss is such a loner that it's hard to talk about a tight alibi. I should have questioned him, but I didn't. I admit I bungled things. I bungled . . . I didn't even question that woman who runs his house. . . ."

"Woman?" Sheppard said, unable to hide his surprise. He looked at Gregory, somewhat obviously trying to restrain a smile. "That's his sister! No, Gregory, the truth is, you haven't accomplished very much. If you didn't want to question her, you should at least have talked to me! The day the body disappeared in Lewes—remember, it was between three and five in the morning—Sciss was at my house."

"At your house?" Gregory whispered.

"Yes. I was trying to talk him into helping us—in a private capacity, of course—and I wanted to show him some of the reports. He left just after midnight—I can't say whether it was five after or twelve-thirty, but even assuming that it was midnight, I doubt whether he could have driven fast enough to get to Lewes before three in the morning. It would have been closer to four. But that's not the most important point. You know, Lieutenant, there are many kinds of improbabilities—material ones, for instance, like the improbability of tossing a coin a hundred times and having it come up heads ninety-nine times. And certain kinds of psychological improbability verge just as closely on the impossible. I've known Sciss for many years. He's an exasperating man, an egomaniac made of razor blades and glass, arrogant in every possible way, absolutely devoid of tact, or perhaps completely unaware that civilized people use good manners not so much out of politeness but for the sake of simple, comfortable coexistence. I have no illusions about him. But the insinuation that he could hide on all fours under some old coffins in a mortuary, or reinforce the jaws of a corpse with adhesive tape, or stamp footprints into the snow, or wrack his brains to figure out how to interrupt rigor mortis, or shake a dead body like a scarecrow to frighten a constable—this is all absolutely incompatible with everything I know about him. Now please try to understand. I don't claim that Sciss couldn't commit a misdemeanor or even a felony. But I'm sure he could never manage a crime that involves such gruesomely crude elements. There can only be one Sciss. Either he's the man who perpetrated that tragic little farce at the cemetery, or he's the man I know. In other words, if Sciss wanted to get away with staging the affair at the cemetery, he'd have to pretend to be completely different in his daily life from the person he really is, or, speaking more cautiously, than the one he may prove to be, if he did everything you accuse him of. Do you think that such consistent role-playing is possible?"

"I've already told you that as far as I'm concerned anything is possible if it frees me from the necessity of believing in miracles," Gregory said in a dull voice, rubbing his palms together as if he suddenly felt cold. "I can't allow myself the luxury of psychologizing. I must have a perpetrator, and I'll get him no matter what the cost. Maybe Sciss is insane—in the full sense of the word—maybe he's a monomaniac, maybe he has a split personality or a divided ego, maybe he has an accomplice, maybe he's using his theory to protect the real culprit—there are more than enough possibilities."

"Answer one question for me," Sheppard said very gently. "But first I want you to understand something: I'm not trying to make suggestions, I'm not initiating anything from the top, and I admit that in this case I don't know anything—not a thing."

"What's the question?" Gregory replied sharply, almost brutally, feeling himself turn pale.

"Why don't you admit that the explanation may not involve criminals?"

"But I've already told you! I've told you several times! Because the only alternative is a miracle!"

"Do you really mean that?" Sheppard asked, his voice suddenly solicitous. "All right, let's leave it for now. The alibi I just gave you for Sciss—you'll check it out, right? I mean the incident at Lewes, because I can only vouch for him up till midnight. My coat is over here, isn't it? Thank you. I think there's going to be a change in the weather; my rheumatism is beginning to act up and it's a bit hard for me to raise my arms. Thank you again. It's after midnight already. I must have lost track of the time. Good night, now. Oh, one more thing. If you have a free moment—for training, so to speak—maybe you ought to do a little detective work around here and let me know who was responsible for that creaking during our conversation. After all, it wasn't a miracle, was it? Please, please, don't look so surprised. You know very well what I'm talking about. Maybe a little too well. Now, if I'm not mistaken, I go out by the staircase on the other side of the drawing room with the mirrors. No, you don't have to show me the way. The door downstairs is locked, but I noticed that the key was still in the lock. You can lock it again later when you get a chance—there aren't any thieves in this neighborhood. Good night again, and above all, Lieutenant, remember—deliberation and discretion."

He went out. Gregory followed him, hardly conscious of what he was doing. The Chief Inspector, not hesitating for a moment, tramped through one room after another and quickly descended the stairs to the front door. The detective followed slowly, hanging on to the bannister like a drunken man. The front door closed quietly. Gregory reached it, locked it, mechanically giving the key two turns, then returned upstairs, his head roaring, his eyes burning as if on fire. Just the way he was, fully dressed, he threw himself down on his bed. The house was still. Through the window some far-off lights were dimly visible. The clock ticked quietly. It would be difficult to say how long Gregory remained in the same position without moving.

After a while the lamp on the desk seemed less bright than before. "I must be very tired," Gregory thought. "I have to get to sleep or I won't be good for anything tomorrow." But he didn't make a move. Something—a tiny cloud or a puff of smoke—floated over the empty armchair in which Sheppard had been sitting. Gregory ignored it and lay there listlessly, listening to his own breathing. Suddenly, the room reverberated with the sound of knocking.

Three separate and quite distinct knocks followed. Gregory turned his head toward the door but still did not get up. Three more knocks. He wanted to say "come in" but couldn't; his mouth hadn't been so dry since his last hangover. Standing up, he made for the door.

Gregory put his hand on the doorknob but was unable to move, suddenly overcome by fear of whoever might be on the other side. Finally, he yanked the door open and, his heart sinking, peered into the darkness. There was no one there. He ran out into the long band of light emanating from the lamp behind him, then made his way past a line of opened doors, his arms extended frontward so he wouldn't bump into whoever it was.

Not encountering anything, Gregory moved farther down the hallway, increasingly enveloped in the resonating sounds. "I never realized this house was so big," he thought; at almost the same moment he saw a tall shadow backing into a side hall. He took off in pursuit; but the light, pattering sound of hurrying feet told him that his quarry was running too. An instant later a door loomed up in front of Gregory. He managed to jump inside just as it slammed shut, nearly crashing into a blue-sheeted bed but stopping himself in time. It was Mr. Fenshawe's room. More confused than ever, he wanted to get away. A bowl-shaped alabaster lamp was hanging so low over the table that it practically touched him. The table itself had been pushed alongside the bed. Farther inside, next to the wall adjacent to his room, he saw two female manikins—the kind used in high-fashion salons—good figures, beautiful features, real hair. They were both naked, their cream-colored limbs glistening in the light of the lamp, and one, gazing at Gregory with an affable fixed smile, was tapping rhythmically on the wall. He was stunned by the sight.

At almost the same instant he saw Mr. Fenshawe sitting on the floor behind the manikin, cackling quietly to himself as if he had a hacking cough. A complicated set of strings ran from his hands to the arms and bodies of both manikins, and the old man, aided by some levers of the kind found backstage at a puppet theater, was manipulating them skillfully.

"No, no," he said, "please don't be frightened. I apologize if the noise keeps you awake, but I can only do this at night. I contact the spirit world, you know."

"But you need a table for that," Gregory said absently, glancing around the room without knowing what he was looking for.

"Tables are old-fashioned. It's done this way now," replied Mr. Fenshawe, not interrupting his manipulation of the strings.

Gregory didn't answer. There was a floor-length, yellow-fringed window drape hanging behind Mr. Fenshawe; it was protruding slightly on one side, as if carefully pulled over a big vertical object of some kind.

Addressing an idiotic question to Mr. Fenshawe—something or other about the manufacture of manikins—then praising the old man's skill in manipulating them, Gregory gradually moved sideways along the wall until he was within touching distance of the drape. He extended his arm and touched a broad, full fold: it gave a little under the pressure, then resisted it. Gregory knew now: someone was hiding behind the drape! He took a deep breath, stood for a second with his muscles tensed, then began walking around the room, keeping up a steady chatter. He confessed to Mr. Fenshawe about his nightly fears; then, uncertain whether he had managed to allay the old man's suspicions, he told him about the investigation, pausing once in front of the manikins and once in front of the drape, addressing himself first to them and then directly to it, as if he was no longer paying any attention to Mr. Fenshawe. These maneuvers made him feel that he was beginning to gain the advantage; well aware of the risks, he began to space his words with double meanings, simultaneously poking at the protruding part of the motionless yellow drape with a feeling of mingled triumph and fear. Laughing out loud, Gregory swept the room with a flashing glance, looking something like a second-rate actor's version of a detective. The cry "Come out! I've got you!" pounded steadily in his head. His speech became blurred and incoherent; in his excitement he blurted out sentences without bothering to complete them. Standing with his back to the drape, Gregory was so close to whoever was hiding behind it that he could feel the warmth of his body. All at once old Mr. Fenshawe jumped up from the floor, an expression of terror and compassion in his eyes, and in the same instant something grabbed hold of Gregory. Unable to tear loose or to breathe, he flapped his arms helplessly; an icy cold sharpness pierced his chest; everything around him stopped, the room became as motionless as a photograph. Gregory fell gently, thinking with extraordinary acuity, "Well, it's over, but why don't I feel anything?—with his last bit of consciousness he prepared himself for the pain, struggling to keep his eyes open. Looking up from the floor, he saw a grayish figure framed by the yellow drape. The man bent over Gregory with uncommon interest. "I can't see," the lieutenant thought in despair. "Now I'll never find out which of the two . . ." Just as Gregory began to understand that the man had killed him, that the contest had ended with his adversary the victor, the room around him became a gigantic noisy bell. And then he woke up . . . in a dark room, with the cold, acrid aroma of tobacco smoke hanging in the air. The telephone was ringing. It stopped for a while, then began again. Only half awake, with a head as heavy as the nightmare itself, Gregory gradually realized that the monotonous ringing had been going on for quite some time.

"Gregory," he stammered into the receiver, leaning with his full weight on an outstretched hand; the room was whirling around.

"This is Gregson. I've been calling you for half an hour. Guess what, pal, a report just came in from Beavers Home. They found that guy's corpse—the one that disappeared about three weeks ago."

"What?" said Gregory in terror. "Where? What corpse?"

"Hey, come on, are you still sleeping? The body of that sailor—Aloney—the one that disappeared from the dissecting lab. They found it in an old iron foundry. In pretty lousy condition too. It must have been there a long time."

"In Beverley?" Gregory asked quietly. His head was throbbing—he felt as if he'd been out on an all-night drunk.

"No, in Beavers Home. Hey, pull yourself together. It's about six miles farther north, where Lord Altringham has his stables. You know where I mean?"

"Who found it?"

"Some workmen; the report just came in but it was last night. In the middle of some junk in front of an old quonset hut. Piles of rusted sheet metal all over the place. You going?"

"No. I can't," Gregory blurted out belligerently, and immediately added in a quiet voice, "I don't feel too well. It may be the flu. Send Calls—you get in touch with him, all right? And a doctor too. Sorensen won't be able to go; that is, he won't want to. Try King. Please take care of it for me, Gregson. Calls will be able to manage everything. Oh, have them take a photographer along. Why am I bothering with all this—you know what to do. I really can't go."

He stopped short, afraid that he was talking too much. For a moment there was silence on the other end.

"Whatever you say," Gregson said at last. "If you're sick, you can't go. I thought you'd be interested."

"I am, of course! I want to know whatever they find out. I'm going to take good care of myself—aspirin, the whole works—I'll be back on my feet soon, and I'll try to get to the Yard around . . . around one. Tell Calls I'll be waiting for him."

Gregory hung up and walked over to the window. It was daybreak; he knew he'd never be able to fall asleep again. He swung open the terrace door and stood in the penetrating damp air. The curtain stirred gently. He stared at the colorless sky of the new day.

6.

It was a few minutes to four when Gregory arrived at the Ritz. Glancing at a clock built into a column marking a streetcar stop, he paused in front of a display of still photographs from a new film and casually studied the glass-covered pictures of a long-legged woman in torn underwear, some masked gangsters, and two cars colliding in a cloud of dust. One after another, big American cars pulled up in front of the restaurant. A pair of tourists from across the ocean emerged from a long black Packard: the woman, old and hideously made up, was wearing diamonds and a sable cape; her escort, a slim young man discreetly dressed in gray, held her handbag and waited patiently until she got out of the car. On the other side of the street the neon marquee of a theater flashed on in a burst of light and movement, its bluish reflection glittering in the windows of nearby stores. When the hands of the clock indicated 4:20, Gregory began moving toward the Ritz. The earlier part of the afternoon had gone as he expected. Calls finally came back with a medical report on the body and an account of the circumstances in which it was found, both absolutely worthless, and Gregory was forced to admit that his idea of setting up stake-outs to watch for the returning bodies was fantasy, plain and simple. He couldn't possibly get enough policemen to cover an area of more than eighty square miles.

A doorman in gold braid opened the door for him. His gloves were more respectable-looking than Gregory's. Uncertain how the meeting would go, the lieutenant was worried and ill at ease. Sciss had phoned him around noon to suggest having dinner together, trying so hard to be gracious that he gave the impression of having forgotten the events of the previous evening. He hadn't even mentioned the unfortunate phone call. "The second act," Gregory mused, looking around the large dining room. He saw Sciss and headed for his table, thus managing to escape from the approaching headwaiter. As he drew closer he saw that there were two other men with Sciss. He didn't recognize either one. When the introductions were over, Gregory leaned uncomfortably against the red velvet upholstered back of his chair; he was flanked on both sides by majolica potted palms, and from the table, which was situated on a raised platform, he had a fine view of the whole interior of the Ritz: elegant women; brilliantly colored, brightly lit fountains; pseudo-Moorish columns. Sciss handed him the menu. Gregory wrinkled his forehead, pretending to study it. He was beginning to feel that Sciss was out to make a fool of him.

His earlier assumption—that Sciss wanted to have a candid private talk—was clearly wrong. "The ass is using his friends to impress me," Gregory thought, looking with affected indifference at his table companions, Armour Black and Doctor McCatt. Gregory knew Black from his books and from pictures in the newspapers. About fifty years old, Black was at the height of his popularity. A long series of best-selling novels, written after years of silence, had finally made him famous. The writer kept himself in excellent shape, and in person it was easy to see that the news pictures showing him on the tennis court or with fishing rod in hand were genuine. Black had big, neatly manicured hands; his head was large, with a thick crop of dark hair, a fleshy nose, and thick eyebrows that overshadowed his face; sometimes, when he closed his eyes for a while in the middle of a conversation, his age showed. The other man seemed much younger but probably wasn't; boyish-looking

152

and very thin, he had close-set blue eyes and a protruding Adams apple that seemed to stretch the skin of his neck. His behavior was eccentric, to say the least. Sometimes he hunched over and stared with glazed eyes at the whiskey glass in front of him; then, seeming to regain his senses, he'd straighten up and sit rigidly for a minute or so. A moment later he would stare around the dining room with his mouth gaping open or would turn, stare persistently at Gregory, then break out laughing like a mischievous child. He seemed the same type as Sciss, and because of this Gregory assumed he was one of Sciss's students. But while Sciss reminded him of a long-legged bird, there was something reminiscent of a rodent in McCatt.

The drift of Gregory's zoological associations was interrupted by a slight dispute between Black and Sciss.

"No, anything but Chateau Margot," the writer stated categorically, shaking the wine list. "That sorry excuse for a wine would kill even the best appetite. It destroys the taste buds and curdles the stomach juices. And in general," he said, glancing at the wine list with an air of aversion, "there's nothing here. Not a thing! Of course it isn't my problem. I'm used to making sacrifices."

"Oh, please." Sciss seemed genuinely embarrassed. The headwaiter appeared, his dignified bearing and long, black tails reminding Gregory of a well-known symphony orchestra conductor. Black was still grumbling when the hors d'oeuvres were served. Sciss tried to make conversation, bringing up a recent news item, but his effort was received in silence. Without making the slightest effort to answer, Black turned to Sciss with his mouth full, his eyes blazing in outrage as if the scientist was guilty of some terrible indiscretion. "This famous friend of his certainly doesn't let him get away with anything," Gregory thought to himself with satisfaction. The men ate silently against the increasingly noisy background of the other diners. Between the soup and the main course, McCatt lit a cigarette, unwittingly threw the burned-out match into his wine, then had some trouble fishing it out. Gregory, for want of anything better to do, watched him listlessly. The meal was nearly over when Black finally spoke.

"All right, I forgive you. But if I were in your place, Harvey, my conscience would be bothering me. That duck—what did they do to her before she died? There's something about long-drawn-out funerals that always ruins the appetite."

"But Armour . . ." Sciss mumbled, uncertain what to say. He tried to laugh but without much success.

Black shook his head slowly. "I didn't say anything. Here we are—vultures gathered from the four corners of the earth . . . and those apples! What an atrocity! To stone a defenseless animal to death with apples! Don't you agree: oh, and à propos, you're compiling statistics on supernatural occurrences in cemeteries, if I remember correctly, aren't you?"

"Yes. I can show them to you if you want. There's nothing supernatural involved. You'll see for yourself."

"Nothing supernatural? How dull! My dear fellow, if there's no element of the supernatural, I'm not at all interested in your statistics. What good are they?"

Observing Sciss's agony and his complete inability to defend himself against Black, Gregory finally began to enjoy himself.

"But it's really a very interesting problem," McCatt observed good-heartedly.

"What problem? Nothing but some plagiarism from the Gospels, that's all! Or is there something I don't know about?"

"Please try to be serious for a minute," Sciss said, making no effort to disguise his impatience.

"But I'm never more serious than when I'm joking," said Black.

"You know," McCatt turned to Sciss, "I'm reminded of a story. You've heard of the Elberfeld horses, haven't you— the ones that were supposed to be able to read and count. The case was very much like the one you're working on— the only alternatives seemed to be fraud or a miracle."

"And in the end it turned out that it wasn't a fraud, right?" Black interrupted.

"No, it wasn't. The man who trained the horses—I can't remember his name—wasn't trying to deceive anyone. He really believed that the horses could talk and count. They tapped out numbers and the letters of the alphabet with their hooves, and they were usually able to hit on the right answer by watching him—not by lip reading or anything like that, but by interpreting various aspects of his outward appearance—changes in his facial expression, unconscious gestures, changes in his posture, movements so slight that human observers didn't notice them. But of course these performances all took place under strict scientific supervision."

"And that explanation satisfied the scientists?"

"Yes, by and large. Because in this case the traditional position that you must choose between two possibilities— *either* a miracle *or* a bluff—didn't work. There was a third answer."

"I have a better analogy," Sciss said, leaning forward on his elbows. "Table tipping. As you know, even people who don't believe in spiritualism can lift tables into the air and move them around. From the traditional point of view, you have either another case of fraud or a genuine manifestation from the spirit world. But in actual fact it isn't a fraud or a spirit that tips the table. The movement results from the combined action of all the microscopic muscle vibrations of each individual in the group of people whose hands are joined above the table. Since each of these individuals is an organism of the same kind, their neuromuscular structures are closely related; thus we see a specific collective process, a definite oscillation of tonus, muscle tension, and nervous impulse rhythm. The people in the circle are completely unaware of the phenomenon, and in effect a combination of forces occurs which brings pressure to bear on the tabletop."

"Oh, come on," said the writer, considerably quieter now and showing real interest. "Exactly what are you trying to say? That the corpses disappeared because of an oscillation in the afterworld? That dead bodies rise from time to time to satisfy a complicated statistical procedure? My dear fellow, I much prefer a miracle without the statistical trimmings."

"Armour, must you make fun of everything?" Sciss flared up angrily, his forehead turning red. "My analogy was elementary and therefore incomplete. This series of so-called resurrections, which really aren't resurrections at all, presents a specific curve. It isn't as if all the corpses disappeared on the same day. The incidents began with very slight body movements, then the phenomenon increased, reached a maximum, and began to drop. So far as the coefficient of correlation with cancer is concerned, it is considerably higher than the coefficient of correlation between sudden deaths and sunspots. I already told you that—"

"I know! I know! I remember! It's a simple case of cancer *à rebours:* instead of killing things it does the opposite —it brings them back to life. A brilliant scheme, symmetrical, positively Hegelian!" said Black. His left eyelid was fluttering impatiently, making it look as if a black butterfly was sitting just under his eyebrow. This impression was heightened by the writer's angry efforts to stop the movements of the tic with his finger.

"Nowadays rationalism is the fashion, not the method, and superficiality is always one of the characteristic features of fashion," Sciss said coldly, ignoring the writer's sarcasm. "At the end of the nineteenth century it was universally believed that we knew almost everything there was to know about the material world, that there was nothing left to do, except keep our eyes open and establish priorities. The stars moved in accordance with calculations not very different from those needed to run a steam engine; the atoms too, and so forth. A perfect society was attainable, and it could be constructed bit by bit according to a clear-cut plan. In the exact sciences these naively optimistic theories were abandoned long ago, but they are still alive in the thought processes of everyday life. So-called common sense relies on programmed nonperception, concealment, or ridicule of everything that doesn't fit into the conventional nineteenth century vision of a world that can be explained down to the last detail. Meanwhile, in actuality you can't take a step without encountering some phenomenon that you cannot understand and will never understand without the use of statistics. And thus we have, for example, the famous *duplicitas causum* of the doctors, the behavior of crowds, and the cyclical fluctuations of the content of dreams, or such phenomena as table tipping."

"Fine, fine. You're right as usual. But what about the cemetery incidents?" Black asked gently. "I've heard you out and table tipping will never be a problem for me again, but unfortunately I can't say the same thing about your resurrections."

Gregory twisted around in his chair, delighted by the writer's comments. He glanced eagerly at Sciss. The scientist, having calmed down a bit, was watching the other men with a slight, almost phony smile; the corners of his small mouth turned downward: as always when he was about to say something momentous, his expression combined helplessness with triumph.

"Not long ago McCatt showed me a new electronic computer that uses human language. When he plugged it in, the speaker gave a few grunts and started babbling incoherently. It sounded like a phonograph record being played at the wrong speed, but with a record you can sometimes recognize snatches of music or words; the sounds the computer produced were all gibberish. It took me completely by surprise—I still remember the experience vividly. Incidentals like that sometimes prevent you from seeing the whole picture. In the case of the mortuaries, the corpses are only accessories, shocking perhaps, but . . ."

"So you still maintain that according to your formula the thing has been solved," said Black slowly, watching through drooping eyes as Sciss emphatically denied the statement with his head.

"Let me finish. My mass-statistical approach concentrates on the phenomenon as a whole. I admit that we still need an analysis of the individual instances, and a study of the processes which generate the actual movements of the dead bodies, but such a particularized, specific treatment of the problem is outside my field of competence."

"Now I understand. You're saying that your theory explains the movement of a large number of bodies taken as a group, but that we still don't know what makes any particular corpse move?"

Sciss compressed his lips, then pouted again. He answered in a quiet voice, but a slight grimace testified to the feeling of contempt behind his words.

"Any event can be understood on two levels, and this is a fact that you won't change by ridiculing me. According to statistics, let's say, a gun is fired once every five days in a big city. But if you're sitting next to a window and a bullet smashes the pane over your head, you don't reason this way: 'A shot has just been fired, there won't be another for five more days, therefore I'm safe.' Instead, you assume that someone is after you with a gun, maybe a madman, and that it's a good idea to take cover under the table. I have just given you an example of the difference between a prediction based on mass-statistics and an individual reaction to a single event; the individual reaction is relatively subordinate to the mass-statistical calculation."

"What do you think about all this?" Black asked, turning to Gregory.

"Me? I'm looking for a human criminal," the lieutenant replied quietly.

"Is that so? Yes, of course . . . naturally, as a specialist in individual occurrences, you wouldn't believe in a virus."

"But I do believe in it. It's a remarkable virus. And fortunately it has many identifiable traits. For example, it likes darkness and solitude, that's why it only operates at night in godforsaken out-of-the-way holes. It avoids policemen like the plague—evidently because they have some special immunity. Furthermore, it likes dead animals, especially cats. And it has literary interests also, although it limits itself to weather forecasts."

The writer listened to Gregory with increasing amusement. His face changed, taking on a cheerful expression, and he began speaking quickly.

"You could get a warrant to arrest almost anyone with that description, Inspector. Whoever throws rocks at the Earth, for instance. After all, meteors usually strike the Earth at night, they come down in solitary places where there are no people or policemen to see them—in fact, they almost always hit a little before daybreak, which shows how tricky they are, since night watchmen usually fall asleep just before dawn. If you asked Sciss about this, he'd tell you that the areas most frequently bombarded by meteors lie in a zone of retreating night and thus constitute the forepart of Earth during its cosmic voyage through space—and, since it is a well-known fact that more falling leaves hit the front window of a moving car than the rear window, we have an analogy . . . et cetera. But you have to find a perpetrator soon, don't you?"

"Falling meteors and viruses acting up don't interest me —I'm concerned about the real person behind all this; I may be unimaginative but he's the only perpetrator I want. I'm not worried about whoever's responsible for meteors and stars. . . ." Gregory answered, his tone sharper than he intended.

The writer watched him for a moment. "Oh, you'll get your man all right. I guarantee it. Besides . . . you already have him."

"Really?" The lieutenant raised his eyebrows.

"It may be that you aren't going after him the right way —maybe you haven't collected enough evidence to put the finger on him yet—but that's not the real point. A culprit who isn't caught is a defeat for you—it means still another folder in the unsolved cases file. But a culprit who doesn't exist, who never existed, that's something completely different, worse than all your records burning up, worse even than confused language in your official reports, it's the end of the world! For you the existence of the perpetrator of a crime has nothing to do with victory or defeat—it's a matter of the sense or absurdity of your profession and your daily activities. And because catching him means peace of mind, salvation, and relief, you'll get him by hook or by crook, you'll get the bastard even if he doesn't exist!"

"In other words, I have a persecution mania, I'm obsessed, I'm proceeding in spite of the facts?" said Gregory, closing his eyes. The conversation had gone on long enough —he was ready to end it even if he had to be arrogant.

"The reporters are all eager to talk to that constable who ran away from the mortuary," said Black. "Are you? Do you expect much from his story?"

"No."

"I knew it," the writer said coldly. "If he recovers and says he saw a resurrection with his own eyes, you'll think he imagined it, you'll tell yourself that you can't depend on the testimony of a man who has a serious brain concussion, and all the doctors will say the same thing. Or maybe you'll say that your perpetrator was even more clever than you assumed—that the constable couldn't see him because he used some kind of invisible nylon thread or covered himself with a black substance. For you, Inspector, only Barabbas exists; if you had been a witness at that famous scene, and heard a voice saying 'Lazarus, arise!'—you'd remain yourself, you wouldn't change at all. By yourself I mean a victim of hallucination or illusion, or a clever fraud. I say that you will never, never give up the idea that there is a perpetrator because your existence depends on his!"

Although he had told himself not to let Black's remarks affect him, Gregory could feel his face turning pale. He tried to smile but couldn't.

"In other words, I'm the kind of policeman who was assigned to guard the Holy Sepulcher," he said. "Or I'm like Paul—before his conversion. You're not going to give me a single break, are you?"

"No!" said the writer. "But it's not me. You yourself won't. This isn't a question of methodology or statistics or even of systematic investigation—it's a matter of faith. You believe in a perpetrator because you have to. We need policemen like you, but we also need Holy Sepulchers."

"I'll go you one better," said Gregory, laughing unnaturally. "You could say that I'm not even doing what I want to do, just acting out a role in a tragedy, or a tragicomedy. Or something, you tell me, since you're so eager to be the chorus . . ."

"Why not? That's my job," the writer declared.

Sciss had been listening to this conversation with growing impatience. Finally, he could no longer contain himself.

"Armour, my dear friend," he said in a persuasive voice,

"paradoxes are as necessary to you as water is to a fish. I know you enjoy doing it, but don't reduce things to absurdities."

"A fish doesn't create the water," Black responded, but Sciss wasn't listening.

"This case has to do with facts, not with drama or lyric poetry. As you know very well, *Entia non sunt multiplicanda.* Faith is not involved in the analysis of a series of facts. A working hypothesis may sometimes be invalid, but even an invalid hypothesis, if nothing else, affirms that there is a human perpetrator. . . ."

"As long as there are human beings facts don't exist in a void," said the writer. "Once a fact emerges into consciousness it is already an interpretation. Facts? A thousand years ago a similar event gave rise to a new religion. And even if it had turned out to be an anti-religion, there would still be the same crowds of believers and priests, the mass hallucinations, the empty coffins pulled apart for relics, the blind seeing, the deaf beginning to hear. . . . I admit that action in this sphere is more limited and less mythologized nowadays, the Inquisitor doesn't threaten to torture anyone for statistical heresies—that's why the tabloid papers make such big profits. Facts, my dear friend, are your business as well as the Inspector's. You're both the kind of disciples on which our era is founded. Inspector, I hope you aren't angry at me because of our little disagreement. I don't know you so I can't possibly predict whether or not you'll end up another Paul. But even if you do, Scotland Yard will remain the same. The police are never converted. I don't know if you ever noticed that."

"You turn everything into a joke," Sciss grunted indifferently. McCatt whispered to him for a moment, then they both got up. Outside the checkroom Gregory found himself standing next to Sciss, who suddenly turned to him and said in a lowered voice:

"Do you have anything to say to me?"

Gregory hesitated, then, acting on an impulse, took Sciss's hand and shook it.

"Please don't think about me, just go about your work in peace," he replied.

"Thank you," said Sciss. His voice was so shaky that even Gregory was surprised and confused. Armour Black's car was parked in front of the Ritz. Sciss got in with him, leaving Gregory alone with McCatt. Although Gregory would have preferred to say good-bye, McCatt proposed that they walk together for a while.

Both men were the same height; walking side by side, they reluctantly became aware of this fact on several different occasions when each discovered the other peering at him curiously out of the corner of his eye. These unexpected encounters called for a smile, but neither one was willing to make the gesture. After a while McCatt stopped at a vegetable stand and bought a banana. Peeling it, he glanced at Gregory.

"Do you like bananas?"

"Not too much."

"Are you in a rush?"

"No."

"Why don't we try our luck," McCatt suggested, pointing at the brightly lit entrance of a penny arcade.

Cheered by the thought, Gregory nodded and followed him inside. Several greasy-haired teenagers were watching sullenly as one of their number fired a line of blue sparks at a small airplane revolving behind the window of a glass case. McCatt walked straight to the back of the arcade, passing a row of pinball machines and automatic roulette games. He stopped in front of a glass-topped metal case. Underneath the glass cover there was a green landscape, complete with bushes and trees. He deftly threw a coin into the slot, pulled a lever, and turned to Gregory.

"Do you know this game?"

"No."

"It's called 'Hottentots and Kangaroo.' There aren't any Hottentots in Australia, but what difference does it make? I'll be the kangaroo. Ready?"

He pressed a button. A little kangaroo jumped out of a black slot and fell into a clump of bushes. Gregory pulled his lever—and three funny-looking little black figures slid out on his side. He manipulated the handgrip, moving his Hottentots closer to the place where he thought the kangaroo was hiding. At the last minute the kangaroo jumped out, broke through Gregory's skirmish line, and again took refuge in the jungle. They wandered that way across the whole plastic map; every time Gregory got too close the kangaroo managed to escape. Finally Gregory worked out a tactical plan: positioning one Hottentot at the place where the kangaroo had disappeared, he held the other two in reserve, aligning them in such a way that McCatt couldn't possibly escape. He caught the kangaroo on his next move.

"For a beginner you're very good," McCatt said. His eyes were sparkling, he was chuckling like a boy. Gregory shrugged his shoulders, feeling somewhat foolish.

"Maybe because I'm a hunter by profession."

"No, it's not that. You have to use your mind in this game. There's no other way to play it. You understood the principle right off. This game lends itself to mathematical analysis, you know. Sciss hates this kind of fun—it's a defect, a fundamental defect in his personality. . . ."

That said, he walked slowly down the row of slot machines, threw a coin into one of them and jerked the lever, setting the colorful disks into motion: a flood of coins streamed out of the machine into his outstretched hand. The kids up front, noticing this, began to move slowly in his direction, watching as McCatt nonchalantly threw the money into his pocket. But McCatt didn't try his luck again and the two men left, passing the stubborn dull-witted fellow near the entrance who was still shoving coin after coin into the machine in a desperate effort to shoot down the airplane.

An arcade lined by shops came into view a few steps farther on. Gregory recognized it at once: it was the same one he had wandered into not long before; inside, toward the back, he saw a huge mirror closing off the far end.

"There's no exit here," he said, coming to a stop.

"I know. You suspect Sciss, don't you?"

Gregory paused for a moment before answering.

"Is he a friend of yours?"

"You could say that. But . . . he really doesn't have any friends."

"I know, it's not very easy to like him," Gregory said with surprising emphasis. "Only . . . you shouldn't ask me questions like that."

"I only meant it rhetorically. After all, it's obvious that you suspect him. Maybe not of engineering the disappearances, but, let's say . . . of being an accomplice. However, and I don't mean to sound facetious, only time will tell. I just want to know one thing: would you close the investigation if you witnessed, with your own eyes, something that looks like a resurrection? That is, a dead man sitting, moving around . . ."

"Did Sciss tell you to ask me that?" Gregory asked in a sarcastic tone of voice. Without realizing it, the two men had walked as far as the center of the arcade, stopping in front of a shop window. Inside it a barefoot window decorator was undressing a willowy blonde manikin. Gregory was suddenly reminded of his dream. He watched attentively as the manikin's slender, pink body emerged from under the gold lamé.

165

"It's too bad you understood it that way," McCatt answered slowly. Bowing his head slightly, he turned on his heel and walked away, leaving Gregory in front of the shop window.

The lieutenant took a few steps farther into the arcade, but turned back after seeing his reflection in the mirror. On the street outside more and more window displays were lit up, and the noise and bustling had intensified as it usually does in the early evening. Continually jostled as he walked along deep in thought, he finally turned into a side street. After a minute or two he found himself standing at the entrance to a courtyard. The display cases on both sides of the gate belonged to a photographer, and his eyes swept over the rows of wedding pictures, quickly taking in the conventionally retouched happy couples—the brides all smiling shyly behind their veils, the tuxedoed men affecting virile poses. He walked into the courtyard. An old man in a slovenly, unbuttoned leather smock was kneeling beside the open hood of an old car, listening to the purring of its motor with his eyes closed. Behind him there was a garage, its doors open. Gregory could see several other cars inside, as well as empty gasoline cans and piles of spare parts scattered along the walls. The man in the smock, seeming to sense Gregory's presence, opened his eyes and jumped to his feet. The expression of ecstasy left his face.

"What can I do for you, mister? You want to rent a car?"

"What? Uh . . . you rent cars?" Gregory asked.

"Of course. Allow me, sir. Would you like a new one? I have this year's Buick, automatic transmission, the smoothest ride you ever had. How long do you want it?"

"No . . . uh, yes. Just for tonight. Yes, I'll take the Buick," Gregory decided. "Do you want a deposit?"

"That depends."

Gregory showed him his identity card. The man smiled and bowed.

"You don't have to leave no deposit, Inspector, it goes without saying. You can pay me the fifteen shillings later. The Buick, right? Should I gas her up?"

"Yes. Will it take long?"

"No . . . only a minute."

The man disappeared into the garage. One of the dark cars gave a start and quietly pulled out onto the concrete drive. Gregory paid, placing the money in the proprietor's chubby, greasy palm. He slammed the door, adjusted the seat, tested the brake, worked the pedals for a moment to get accustomed to them, threw the car into gear, and drove carefully into the street. It was still fairly light outside.

The car was really new and it handled easily. At the first red light Gregory turned around and studied its length through the panoramic rear window. He wasn't used to such a big car, but he enjoyed the rhythmic throbbing of its powerful engine. The traffic was heavy for a while, but Gregory put on more speed after it thinned out. There were fewer private cars in the street now, and more brightly painted vans, panel trucks, and motorcycles delivering merchandise. He had reached the East End when he realized that he didn't have any cigarettes.

Gregory drove along several narrow streets posted with no parking signs, finally finding a spot next to a cluster of dry trees enclosed by an old iron grating that looked like a huge bird cage. He backed the Buick in until he could feel the tires bumping gently against the curb, then got out and began looking for a tobacco shop he had seen from the car. He had never been in this neighborhood before, however, and as a result he couldn't find it. He walked up the next side street. It was beginning to get darker. He saw two or three long-haired youths loitering in the glare outside a small movie house. Their hands crammed into the pockets of their wrinkled tight pants, they were patiently watching the still photographs in a revolving drum that advertised coming attractions. Just past the movie theater Gregory was caught in a blast of hot air from the open door of a cafeteria. Inside he could see some sausages sizzling on an open grill, and through the smoke he made out several more long-haired characters like the ones outside the theater. Finally he found the tobacco shop. The proprietor, a short hunchback with a face as flat as a pancake and almost no neck, handed him a package of American cigarettes. On the way out Gregory encountered another dwarf; this one, unusually fat, with short arms and legs, was removing a tray of sugar-covered pastries from a delivery wagon. Gregory tore the cellophane off the package, lit a cigarette, and inhaled deeply. Deciding to return to the car by a different route, he crossed the street and walked straight ahead, looking for a cross street leading to the right. He passed another cafeteria, its door open also, with a narrow, sausage-shaped red, green, and white flag drooping over its entrance like a rag. Down the street there was a penny arcade full of people, a grocery, and a hardware store. Most of the sidewalk outside the hardware store was blocked by piles of merchandise. The proprietor, dressed in a black sweater and smoking a pipe, was sitting under a tree, watching a little cart on the other side of the street. Hearing a catchy tune from that direction, Gregory paused and took a close look. Although the occupant of the cart was standing, only the upper part of his chest was visible; actually, it was an armless torso; the head, swinging to left and right in quick half turns was playing a brisk march on a harmonica mounted on a wire frame. Gregory put his hand in his pocket and toyed nervously with a coin; then, by an effort of sheer willpower, forced himself to walk away. The high-pitched sound of the harmonica followed him for a while. Shuddering as the image of the street musician flashed into his mind, Gregory realized, almost as an afterthought, that he was beginning to feel a little like a dwarf. The idea fascinated him. "A street of dwarfs," he thought. It suddenly occurred to him that the series of disappearances had to have a clear-cut meaning, even if it was hidden. It would be difficult to discard everything at this point and start all over again on a hunch, he mused. There were no street lamps and it was getting darker and darker—the street was lit only by faint streaks of light from the shop windows. Up ahead Gregory saw a gap in the streaks—the street he was looking for.

The cross street was almost empty, lit more or less by an old-fashioned gas lamp hanging from a spiral iron arm attached to a wall. Gregory walked slowly, smoking his cigarette until the wet tobacco at the end began burning and singed his lips. Just past the corner there was an antique shop, or so the sign claimed, but there was nothing in the window except a dusty pile of cardboard boxes and some old photographs of movie stars scattered about like an abandoned deck of playing cards. At the end of the street he found the little square where he had parked the car.

Some children were playing hide-and-seek near the iron grating, popping out from behind the cagelike structure, which enclosed a statue of someone in a bishop's miter, to throw pieces of wood at his Buick.

"That's enough fooling around, you hear me!" he shouted, emerging from the shadows. The children scattered noisily, more exuberant than frightened. He got in and started the motor. Cut off from his surroundings by the car windows, he had a premonition that he was about to unleash something he'd be sorry for later on. The premonition urged him not to go ahead with whatever it was he had just started. He hesitated for a second, but his fingers tightened automatically on the gearshift, and the car began coasting down the slope. Reducing speed gradually, he turned into a broad avenue, passing a street sign but not managing to read it.

The dashboard clock radiated a pinkish color; its hands

stood at seven o'clock. Time was really flying today. Various events connected with the case came to mind, but Gregory rejected them—he wanted to push them out of his consciousness, trying hard not to think about the case, as if it was important not to think about it, as if everything would turn out all right if he left it alone; somehow, he felt, all the details would fall into place when he came back to them later on.

He was leaving the East End when the flashing directional signal of a dark car in front of him caught his eye. Recognizing the dented rear bumper, he slowed down and stayed at a safe distance behind the car. He managed without any trouble.

The dark gray sedan turned again into a deserted tree-lined street. Gregory allowed it to get a few more yards ahead; then, to keep from attracting attention, he turned off his lights, following the other car like this for a long time. Once or twice, at intersections, he had to speed up to make sure he wouldn't lose it but he preferred not to get too close. There weren't many other cars on the street though, and Sciss was a careful driver, who used his directional signals often. The orange flashes were a big help, but Gregory was a little annoyed because he didn't always know where he was. Suddenly he recognized the bluish letters of an advertising sign and immediately everything fell into place. There was a branch of the City Bank, next door to it a small cafe he had frequented in his youth. The dark sedan pulled up to the curb. Gregory made a quick decision: at the risk of losing Sciss, who was already getting out of his car, Gregory drove up to the next block. He stopped in front of a big chestnut tree which protected the Buick from the light of the street lamps, slammed the doors, and hurried back, but Sciss was nowhere to be seen. Gregory stopped in front of the cafe and tried to peek through the windows. Some posters pasted on the glass blocked his view, so he raised his collar and went inside, unable to resist the unpleasant feeling that he was doing something ridiculous.

The cafe had several rooms; three or four, he'd never known quite how many. They were spacious, furnished with marble-topped tables; each room was separated from the others by a partition padded with worn-out red velvet, the kind of material used to upholster settees.

Gregory spotted Sciss's reflection in a narrow mirror on the wall of the passageway between the first and second rooms. He was seated at a table, saying something to a waiter. Gregory backed up, looking for a corner from which he could watch Sciss without being seen. It wasn't easy. When he finally selected a spot and sat down, he discovered that the partitions blocked his view of Sciss's table, but he couldn't move because the waiter was already headed toward him. Ordering a hot toddy, Gregory spread out the *Sunday Times*, annoyed that he couldn't see Sciss and that he was sitting like a dog outside a fox's lair. He forced himself to work on the crossword puzzle, watching the empty space between the partitions and the opposite wall. About ten minutes later, while he was still sipping the sickeningly sweet drink, Sciss suddenly stood up and walked quickly from room to room as if looking for someone. Gregory barely managed to hide himself behind the outspread *Times*, but Sciss didn't notice the lieutenant and returned to his "box," now sitting in such a way that Gregory could see his long legs and his bluish yellow shoes. Another ten minutes went by. In the back, near the billiard table, some students were arguing noisily with each other. Sciss leaned out of his hiding place every time the door creaked. Finally, he stood up, smiling heartily at a girl standing in the doorway. She hesitated, then walked toward him, her flat handbag, hanging on a strap from her shoul-

171

der, bouncing against her hips. She was wearing a purple coat, with a hood that covered all but a few wisps of her light-colored hair. Gregory couldn't see her face. The girl stood in front of Sciss, who began talking very rapidly. He touched the sleeve of her coat. She shook her head as if saying no, then slid in between the partition and the table. Both disappeared from view. Taking advantage of a temporary commotion among the students in the back room, Gregory reluctantly circled the inside of the cafe, and headed back to his table from the other direction, attempting all the while to watch Sciss and the girl through a mirror hanging high on the wall. Pretending to be looking for a particular newspaper, he moved from table to table until he found a good vantage point, then fell into a red settee with protruding springs. It was hard to see the mirror, but at least the dim lighting and the location gave some assurance that Sciss wouldn't be able to spot him. The mirror enabled Gregory to see Sciss slightly from above. Sciss had moved from his chair to the sofa next to the girl; talking rapidly, without even looking at her, he almost seemed to be directing his words at the table, an impression heightened by Gregory's foreshortened view of the scene. The girl, full-lipped with a childlike face, was no more than seventeen years old. She still had her coat on, but she had opened it and pushed the hood back, letting her hair spill out over her shoulders. Sitting straight up with her shoulders pressed against the red upholstery, and staring frontward instead of at Sciss, she looked unnaturally stiff and still, conveying the unmistakable impression that she was uncomfortable and perhaps a little tired. Sciss kept talking and talking; at one point he leaned toward the girl, reluctantly pulled back as if his advance had been rejected, then brought his restless thin lips close to her face without looking at her. At the same time, his bony hand moved up and down on the table top in rhythm with what he was saying; clenching and unclenching his fingers, he almost furtively caressed the table. The whole scene was so stupid, so pathetic that Gregory wanted to turn away, but he kept watching. The girl smiled once, but only with her lips, not with her eyes, then continued sitting as before, her head bowed, listening but not saying anything. Gregory could see her in the mirror; her cheeks were cast in shadow by her hair, she had a small, snub nose. For an instant, but only that once, Gregory noticed a sparkle in her eyes. Sciss finally became silent. With his shoulders hunched over and a strained expression on his face, he seemed to be alone even though the girl was still sitting at his side. Staring at the marble table top, he reached for a paper napkin, quickly jotted a few words on it, folded the paper in four parts, and slid it across the table. The girl didn't want to take it. Sciss quite visibly begged and pestered her. She finally picked it up, then put it down again, unopened, touching him with her fingertips. Sciss grabbed her by the hand. She stiffened, glancing at him with wide-open eyes. It seemed to Gregory that her face had darkened. Sciss listened to whatever she was saying, nodded his head, then leaned toward her and began talking slowly, emphatically, underlining words with gestures of his hand, pressing strongly, urgently on the table as if trying to smash something into the slab of marble with his palm. When he finished, he took hold of the edge of the table with both hands as if he wanted to push it away. The girl's lips moved. Gregory read them: "No." Sciss swung around in his chair, turning his face toward the room. Gregory tried to see what had happened to the napkin; it was under the table next to the girl's foot. Meanwhile, Sciss got up. He put a few coins on the table and slowly made his way to the door. He stopped there. The girl followed, pulling the hood over her head without bothering to arrange her hair. She was slender, in a childlike way, with a teenager's long legs. The door hadn't even closed behind them when Gregory was up on his feet; he moved quickly to their table, bent down to pick up the napkin, shoved it into his pocket, and rushed out into the street. The sedan was just beginning to pull away from the curb. The girl was sitting next to Sciss. Without trying to hide, Gregory hurried up the block to his Buick. While struggling with the door lock, he turned around and saw the bright wink of the Chrysler's directional signals disappearing around a corner—Sciss had made a turn. Gregory jumped into his car, stepped on the gas, and pulled away in pursuit—for a while it looked as if he had lost the Chrysler, and he was beginning to feel a sense of relief and satisfaction, but suddenly he caught sight of the gray sedan in the heavy traffic in front of him. Sciss drove onto the upper level of the northbound highway, but at the third exit turned off onto a winding overpass. Gregory followed close behind—the traffic was so heavy that he could allow himself this luxury without being noticed. He attempted to see through the sedan's rear window but couldn't make out much more than two human figures. Before long they arrived in a neighborhood occupied almost entirely by brand-new multistoried housing projects. Sciss came to a sudden stop without pulling over to the curb. Gregory, not wanting to lose him, drove slowly past, then turned around in his seat to watch through his rear window. Sciss unexpectedly accelerated, overtook and passed Gregory's car, made a U-turn, and drove back in the direction he'd come from, leaving Gregory behind. The street ran alongside the project, following a line of six-story buildings and smaller houses set in a sprawling grassy area surrounded by hedges and wire fences. With Gregory some distance behind him again, Sciss drove into a broad parking lot and got out of the car after the girl. Gregory followed them with his eyes until they disappeared in the semidarkness, trying unsuccessfully to locate them in the faint light of the whitish globes over the building entrances. Meanwhile, a passing consta-

174

ble, noticing that its parking lights were on, stopped next to Sciss's car, looked it over carefully with a disapproving expression, then continued on his rounds. Although more than five minutes had gone by, Gregory waited patiently, feeling sure, without knowing why, that Sciss would be back soon enough after failing to achieve his purpose. He got out of the car and strolled along the sidewalk at a leisurely pace until he heard footsteps approaching. It was Sciss coming back: his coat was unbuttoned and he was bareheaded; his hair, standing up around his ears in the strong wind, looked like a pair of bat's wings. Gregory got back into the car, leaving the door slightly open because he didn't want to attract Sciss's attention by slamming it. Overwhelmed by an urgent desire to smoke, he watched Sciss while searching in his pockets for a package of cigarettes. Sciss stood next to his car for a long time, his arms dangling limply at his sides, then traced a pattern on the hood with his fingers as if checking to see if it was dusty. He finally got in and turned off the lights. Gregory immediately started his motor and waited. Sciss didn't move. Gregory put the car in neutral; suddenly reminded of the napkin, he pulled it out of his pocket, unfolded it, and, not wanting to turn his lights on, held it close to the dashboard, barely able to make the words out in the soft glow of the dials and gauges. It was Sciss's address, phone number, and name. It occurred to Gregory that Sciss might be waiting while the girl changed her clothes, but he rejected the thought at once: he was quite certain that Sciss wasn't waiting for anything and didn't expect anything. The dashboard clock showed nine. They'd been sitting this way for a half hour already. Gregory smoked two cigarettes, throwing the butts out the window. He fiddled around with the radio for a while, then, his patience exhausted, got out, slammed the door ostentatiously, and walked over to Sciss's car. Just before reaching it, however, he hesitated, and walked on past.

175

Sciss was slumped against the steering wheel with his face cradled in his arms. A beam of light from a street lamp, partly cut off by the roof of the car, shined on his silvery hair, making a bat's wing pattern on his temple. Gregory stood watching him, not certain what to do. Suddenly he backed away, returned to the Buick as quietly as possible, and, taking a careful look to make sure nothing was moving in Sciss's car, got in and quickly drove away. He made a left turn, went around in a wide circle, and headed back to the same place at high speed. The dark mass of the Chrysler suddenly loomed before him; just as a collision seemed unavoidable he stepped hard on the brake and squealed to a short jerky stop, ramming solidly into Sciss's rear bumper with a metallic grating sound. He jumped out and ran over to the Chrysler.

"I'm terribly sorry," he called out. "My brakes didn't hold. I hope I didn't do too much damage. Oh, it's you," he said quietly.

Sciss, who had been thrown forward by the impact, opened his door, extended one leg as if about to get out but didn't, and instead stared at Gregory, who was affecting a stupid expression.

"You? How did you . . . Gregory, huh? What is this— the police making trouble for law-abiding citizens?" he said.

They walked around to inspect the rear of the car; it was undamaged; as Gregory had planned, the impact had been absorbed by the bumpers.

"Exactly how did you manage to do this?" Sciss asked, straightening himself up.

"I'm driving a rented car and I'm not used to the brakes," Gregory explained. "To tell the truth, I always drive that way—it's a weakness of mine, probably because I'm unfulfilled in some way. You see, I don't have a car of my own."

Deciding that he was probably talking too much, Gregory abruptly became silent.

"You don't have a car?" Sciss repeated. He spoke mechanically, his mind on something else. He pulled on his right glove, buttoned it, and slowly rolled up his left glove. The two men stood side by side next to the cars.

"I'll invite him now," Gregory decided.

"No, I don't," he said. "Poverty is a virtue, so we make a point of being diligent about it in the police department. Look, this was all my fault. Maybe it's in the stars for us to spend the evening with each other since we started it by having dinner together. It's supper time, why don't we have something to eat?"

"Maybe in a cafeteria, considering the poverty," Sciss mumbled. He looked up and down the street as if searching for someone.

"I'm not that poor. How about a moonlight drive to the Savoy? What do you say? They have a few quiet tables up on the balcony, and the wine there is very good."

"No, thank you. I don't drink. I can't. I don't know." Sciss got back in the Chrysler and said quite calmly, "It's all the same to me."

"So you'll come. Wonderful. You go first, I'll follow, all right?" Gregory spoke quickly, pretending to think the scientist had accepted his invitation. Sciss scrutinized him carefully, leaned out of the car as if to get a better look at his face, then slammed the door without warning and pushed the starter. Sitting behind the wheel of his own car, Gregory had no idea whether Sciss was going to head for the Savoy and, pulling out after the Chrysler, he began to hope that he wouldn't. But at the first intersection he realized that Sciss was indeed going to have supper with him.

The drive to the Savoy took less than ten minutes. They left both cars in the parking lot and went inside; it was about nine-thirty. An orchestra was playing on the mezzanine; the dance floor, on a rotating platform in the center of the room, was illuminated from underneath by colored lights. Passing through a row of columns, the two men made their way upstairs. The balcony afforded an excellent view of the whole nightclub, except where the line of sight was impeded by chandeliers hanging from the ceiling. Gregory ignored the waiter, who was trying to lead them to a back table already occupied by a group of noisy people, and, with Sciss behind him, headed for the far end of the balcony, where he found a small table standing by itself between two columns. Two waiters in full dress immediately stepped over to them, one holding the menu, the other the wine list; the list was very thick.

"Do you know wines?" Sciss asked, closing the leather-bound menu. Gregory smiled.

"A little. How about some Vermouth for a start? Do you take it with lemon?"

"Vermouth? Vermouth is too bitter. Oh, never mind. I'll try the lemon."

Gregory nodded to the waiter—it wasn't necessary to say a word. The second waiter stood patiently a short distance away. Gregory deliberated carefully before ordering, making sure to ask Sciss if he liked salads and if fried foods agreed with him.

Leaning toward the railing, Sciss stared without much interest at the whirling heads below. The orchestra was playing a slow fox-trot.

Gregory watched the dancing for a while, then held his glass of Vermouth up to the light.

"There's something I have to tell you," he said, speaking with difficulty. "I . . . owe you an apology."

"What?" Sciss looked up with a distracted expression. "Oh," he said, thinking he understood what Gregory meant. "No, no. Don't mention it. It's not worth making a fuss."

"I know now why you left your post with the General Staff."

"So you know," Sciss said indifferently. He downed his Vermouth in three gulps as if it was tea. The piece of lemon ended up in his mouth; he removed it, held it in his fingers for a moment, then put it back into the empty glass.

"Yes."

"It's no secret. I'm surprised you didn't know all along since you did everything but put me under a microscope. . . ."

"The stories that circulate about someone like you are always contradictory," Gregory continued, as if he hadn't heard Sciss's last remark. "And it's all either hot or cold, there's no in-between. Everything depends on the informant. Maybe you'd like to tell me. Why did they take the Operations command away from you?"

"And label me red," Sciss added. Despite Gregory's eager interest, he didn't seem any more lively. Hunched over in his chair, he leaned an arm on the railing. "Why do you want to know?" he asked at last. "It doesn't make any sense to dig all this up."

"Did you really predict some kind of holocaust?" Gregory asked in a lowered voice. "Please, this is very important to me. You know how people distort and twist everything. Tell me what really happened."

"What difference does it make to you?"

"Frankly, I want to find out exactly who you are."

"That's an old story," Sciss said despondently, still squinting at the dancers downstairs. The naked shoulders of the women on the dance floor were bathed in red light. "No, it has nothing to do with a holocaust. Do you really want to know?"

"Very much so."

"You're that curious? It was sometime around 1946. The nuclear race was just beginning. I knew that sooner or later a saturation point would be reached—I mean the achievement of maximum destructive force. Then a means of delivering the bombs would be developed . . . that is, missiles. This had to reach the saturation point also . . . both sides armed with thermonuclear missiles, the control panels on both sides safely hidden, each one with its infamous button ready. Push the button and the missiles move. Twenty minutes later, the end of the world, both sides—*finis mundi ambilateralis* . . ."

Sciss smiled. The waiter brought a bottle of wine, uncorked it, and poured a few drops into Gregory's glass. Gregory tasted it, wet his lips, and nodded his head.

The waiter filled both glasses and walked away.

"That was your opinion in '46?" Gregory asked, toasting Sciss. The latter tasted the ruby liquid with the tip of his tongue, sipped it carefully, then emptied the glass in one gulp, took a deep breath, and, with a look that was either surprise or embarrassment, put his glass back on the table.

"No, those were only premises. Don't you understand? Once the race begins, it can't stop. It has to go on. If one side invents a big gun, the other retaliates with a bigger one. The sequence concludes only when there is a confrontation; that is, war. In this situation, however, confrontation would mean the end of the world; therefore, the race must be kept going. Once they begin to escalate their efforts, both sides are trapped in an arms race. There must be more and more improvements in weaponry, but after a certain point weapons reach their limit. What can be improved next? Brains. The brains that issue the commands. It isn't possible to make the human brain perfect, so the only alternative is a transition to mechanization. The next stage will be a fully automated headquarters equipped with electronic strategy machines. And then a very interesting problem arises, actually two problems. McCatt called this to my attention. First, is there any limit on the development of these brains? Fundamentally they're similar to computers that can play chess. A computer that anticipates an opponent's strategy ten moves in advance will always defeat a computer that can think only eight or nine moves in advance. The more far-reaching a brain's ability to think ahead, the bigger the brain must be. That's one."

Sciss spoke faster and faster. Gregory sensed that he had already forgotten everything, including to whom he was speaking. He poured some wine. Sciss played with his glass for a while, moving it back and forth along the tablecloth and tipping it over precariously. Suddenly, he picked it up and drained it in one gulp. Downstairs, the dance floor was immersed in yellow light and mandolins were crooning a Hawaiian melody.

"Strategic considerations dictate the construction of bigger and bigger machines, and, whether we like it or not, this inevitably means an increase in the amount of information stored in the brains. This in turn means that the brain will steadily increase its control over all of society's collective processes. The brain will decide where to locate the infamous button. Or whether to change the style of infantry uniforms. Or whether to increase production of a certain kind of steel, demanding appropriations to carry out its purposes. Once you create this kind of brain you have to listen to it. If a Parliament wastes time debating whether or not to grant the appropriations it demands, the other side may gain a lead, so after a while the abolition of parliamentary decisions becomes unavoidable. Human control over the brain's decisions will decrease in proportion to the increase in its accumulated knowledge. Am I making myself clear? There will be two growing brains, one on each side of the ocean. What do you think a brain like this will demand first when it's ready to take the next step in the perpetual race?"

"An increase in its capability," Gregory said in a low voice, watching the scientist through half-closed eyelids. An

181

unexpected silence prevailed downstairs for a moment, followed by an outburst of applause. A woman's voice began singing. A young man in tails set up a small side table on which the waiters placed a tray full of silver serving dishes: carefully heated plates, napkins, and silverware followed.

"No," Sciss answered. "First it demands its own expansion—that is to say, the brain becomes even bigger! Increased capability comes next."

"In other words, you predict that the world is going to end up a chessboard, and all of us will be pawns manipulated in an eternal game by two mechanical players."

Sciss's facial expression was arrogant. "Yes. Only I'm not predicting, I'm drawing conclusions. We are already at the end of the first stage and the rate of escalation is beginning to increase. All this smacks of the improbable, I admit. But it's happening, believe me. It is."

"Yes . . ." Gregory murmured. He leaned across his plate. "Uh . . . what would you suggest . . . about all this?"

"Peace at any price. You may find this odd, but all things considered it seems to me that even extermination would be a lesser evil than the chess game. I'm only drawing conclusions. I don't have any illusions. That's pretty awful, you know . . . not to have illusions." Sciss poured himself some more wine. Reluctantly, almost compulsively, he kept drinking. Gregory didn't have to worry about keeping his glass filled. Downstairs, the orchestra started playing again. A couple walked past their table: the man was swarthy with a thin mustache, the paleness of his face emphasized by the bluish streaks of his beard. The girl, very young, had a white stole over her bare shoulders; it was embroidered with gold threads the same color as her hair. Sciss watched as they went by, staring at the girl with his lips contorted in a pained expression. He pushed his plate away, closed his eyes, and hid his hands under the tablecloth. It looked to Gregory as if he was checking his own pulse rate.

"And what shall we do next on this lovely evening that began so splendidly?" Sciss said after a while, raising his eyelids. Smoothing down his gray hair around his ears, he straightened up in his chair. Gregory crossed the silverware on his plate. The waiter came over at once.

"Would you like some coffee?" Gregory asked.

"Yes, good idea," Sciss agreed. He kept his hands hidden under the tablecloth.

"I think I'm drunk . . ." he smiled in embarrassment, looking around with a surprised, uncertain expression.

"It does you good every once in a while," Gregory said, pouring only for himself.

The coffee was hot and strong. They drank it in silence. It was stuffy and getting stuffier. Gregory looked around for the waiter and, not seeing him, stood up. He found him behind a column near the bar and asked to have the windows opened. By the time he got back to the table a cool, delicate whiff of air was already moving the steam rising above their coffee cups. Sciss was still in his chair, leaning against the railing, his red eyes drooping. He was breathing heavily and the small hard veins of his temple were protruding.

"Do you feel all right?" Gregory asked.

"I can't take alcohol," Sciss said with his eyes closed. "That is, my organism can't. My insides are all muddled, simply muddled, that's all."

"I'm sorry," said Gregory.

"Oh, it's nothing," Sciss kept his eyes closed. "Let's not talk about it."

"Were you against a preventive war? I mean back in '46."

"Yes. But no one really believed it would work, even the people who were advocating it. There wasn't any psychological readiness at the time. We were all under the spell of a universal peace euphoria. You know, if you proceeded gradually, you could lead anyone—even the College of Cardinals—into the practice of cannibalism. But you must move slowly, step by step. Exactly like now."

"What did you do then?"

"Various things. I started many things but actually wasn't able to finish any of them. I was the proverbial stone on which the scythes were sharpened, you see, and nothing much ever comes from that. I won't finish this last case either. I always run into a dead end. Bah, if only I believed in determinism . . . but with me it's all due to a character defect—I can't compromise."

"You're not married, are you?"

"No."

Sciss gave Gregory a suspicious look.

"Why do you ask?"

Gregory shrugged his shoulders.

"Simply . . . I wanted to know. Excuse me if—"

"Outmoded institution . . ." Sciss muttered. "I don't have any children either, if you want all the details. Well, maybe if they could be created intellectually . . . I don't care too much for this genetic lottery, you see. It looks like I'm your guest—shall we leave now?"

Gregory paid. As they were going down the stairs the orchestra bid them farewell with some ear-piercing jazz. They had to slip around the edge of the dance floor, jostled by the dancing couples. Once through the revolving doors, Sciss, with a sigh of relief, took a deep breath of cool air.

"Thank you . . . for everything," he said languidly. Gregory followed him to the cars. Sciss had some trouble finding the key in his pocket. He opened the door, unbuttoned his coat, then took it off and threw it onto the back seat. He sat down behind the steering wheel. Gregory stood beside the car.

Sciss didn't close the door and didn't move.

"I can't drive . . ." he said.

"Move over, I'll drive you," Gregory offered.

He bent down to get in.

"But what about your car?"

"Don't be ridiculous. I can come back for it."

Gregory got in, slammed the door, and quickly pulled away from the parking spot.

7.

Leaving the empty car in the courtyard, Gregory returned to the lobby. Sciss was leaning on the bannister of the staircase with his eyes half-closed, a vague, pained smile playing about his lips. Gregory waited without saying good night. Breathing deeply—it sounded like a sigh—Sciss suddenly opened his eyes. The two men stared at each other.

"I don't know," Sciss said at last. "Do you have . . . time?"

Gregory nodded his head and quietly followed him up the stairs. Neither spoke. Outside his apartment Sciss stopped with his hand on the doorknob as if he wanted to say something; finally he swung the door open.

"It's dark inside, let me go first," he said.

There was a light on in the foyer. The kitchen door was open but there was no one there, only a tea kettle whistling quietly on a low flame. They hung up their coats.

The living room, bathed in light from a white globe on the ceiling, had a neat, festive look. The wall behind the desk was lined with bookshelves; pens and pencils were arranged symmetrically on the desk; a glass table stood just below the bookshelves, with two low green club chairs, their bluish cushions decorated in a geometric pattern, pushed next to it. The table was set with cups, whiskey glasses, trays of fruit and pastries. Spoons, forks—everything was arranged for two people. Sciss rubbed his bony, arthritic hands.

"Why don't you sit down next to the shelves where it's more comfortable," he said with perhaps a little too much liveliness. "I had a guest this afternoon—let me offer you some of the leftovers."

Gregory wanted to say something lighthearted to help Sciss out, but nothing came to mind. He moved one of the chairs and sat down on the arm, turning toward the books.

He found himself facing an impressive multilingual collection of scientific literature—one shelf was filled with works on anthropology, a plastic card attached to the next shelf had the word "Mathematics" written on it. Out of the corner of his eye he noticed some photographs in an open drawer of the desk, but when he turned in their direction, Sciss moved—or, rather, practically hurled himself across the room on his long legs—hitting the drawer with his knee and noisily slamming it.

"A mess, it's a mess," he explained with a tense look. He rubbed his hands again and seated himself on the radiator next to the window.

"Your new attempt to find me guilty is just as half-baked as your last one," he said. "You try too hard. . . ."

"You've had several bad experiences," Gregory commented. He picked a thick volume at random and flipped the pages; algebraic formulas leaped past his eyes.

"Quite true. Do you prefer coffee or tea?" Sciss remembered his responsibilities as a host.

"I'll take whatever you're having."

"Good."

Sciss went into the kitchen. Gregory put back the book, which was entitled *Principia Mathematica,* and stared at the closed desk drawer for a moment. He was tempted to take a look inside but didn't dare. The sound of Sciss bustling about in the kitchen could be heard through the open door. After a few minutes the scientist came back with the tea, poured it into the cups in a high, narrow stream, and sat down opposite Gregory.

"Be careful, it's hot," he cautioned. "Are you saying that

I'm no longer under suspicion?" he asked Gregory after a moment. "You know something? I could have had motives you never even considered. Let's say I was trying to get rid of a body—someone I killed, just for the sake of argument. In order to bring about a situation in which it was easy to dispose of it, I got hold of a whole batch of bodies, began moving them around, and created a general confusion in which my victim was lost completely. What do you say to that?"

"Too literary," Gregory replied. He was browsing through a thick, glossy-paged volume on psychometrics. "One of Chesterton's stories has the same plot."

"I never read it. I don't like Chesterton. In your opinion, then, what made me do all this?"

"I don't know. I can't think of any possible motive. That's why I don't suspect you anymore."

"Did you dig into my past? Did you draw up a chronology and a map showing all my movements? Did you look for clues and fingerprints? With only one exception, I wasn't at all inconvenienced by your investigation—I didn't even notice it."

"The overall picture didn't fall into place so I skipped the usual routine. Besides, I'm not a very systematic investigator. I improvise, or, you might say, I tend to be disorderly," Gregory admitted. There was something stiff in among the pages of the book; he began turning them carefully. "I even have a theory to justify my careless work habits: until you have a specific theoretical structure to fit the facts into, there's no point in collecting evidence."

"Are you an intuitionist? Have you ever read Bergson?"

"Yes."

The pages opened. Between them there was a large photographic negative. It was transparent, but by pressing it against the white paper Gregory was able to make out the silhouette of a human figure bent backward. Very slowly he raised the book closer to his eyes, peeping over it at Sciss. With one finger he moved the negative along the blank area between two columns of print, continuing the conversation at the same time:

"Sheppard told me you were at his place when the body in Lewes disappeared. So you have an alibi. I was acting like a dog looking for a buried bone—running from tree to tree and digging, even though there was nothing there. I was fooling myself. There was nothing for me to dig in, no grounds, nothing. . . ."

Gregory systematically moved the photo along the white strip between the columns until he could make out the image on the negative. It was a picture of a naked woman leaning back against a table. One arm, resting against a stack of black bricks that reached almost to her nipple, was partly covered by her dark, flowing hair—light-colored, in reality. Her long legs stretched down from the table, entwined in a string of white beads. In her other hand she was holding a blurred object of some kind, pressing it against her black, tightly closed thighs. Her lips were open in an indescribable grimace that exposed her dark pointed teeth.

"I think I've already made myself enough of a fool in front of you," Gregory continued.

He glanced suddenly at Sciss. The latter, smiling faintly, nodded his head.

"I don't know. You present another point of view. If we were living at the time of the Inquisition you might have gotten what you wanted."

"What does that mean?" Gregory asked. He took another quick look at the negative and suddenly realized that the beads were really a small chain. The girl's ankles were shackled. Frowning, he slammed the book shut, put it back in its place, and eased himself gently from the arm into the chair.

"I have very little resistance to pain, you know," Sciss

190

continued. "Torture would squeeze every bit of evidence out of me. You would probably have broken every bone in my body to save your peace of mind—or, I should say, to maintain your mental equilibrium."

"I understand Sheppard about as much as I do this case," Gregory said slowly. "He assigned me to a hopeless job, and at the same time, right from the beginning, he didn't give me a chance. But you're probably not interested in any of this."

"As a matter of fact, I'm not." Sciss put his empty cup down on the table. "I did what I could."

Gregory stood up and began to walk around the room. On the opposite wall there was a framed photograph, a large-sized picture of a work of sculpture, a good amateur study of light and shadow effects.

"Did you do this?"

"Yes."

Sciss didn't turn his head.

"It's very good."

Sweeping his eyes around the room, Gregory recognized the desk as the table in the negative. Those bricks—they were books, he thought. He checked the windows; quite ordinary, except that they were provided with black shades, now raised and tightly rolled.

"I didn't think you had any artistic interests," he said, returning to the small table. Sciss blinked and got to his feet with a certain amount of difficulty.

"I used to amuse myself with that kind of thing a long time ago. I have quite a few pictures like that one; would you like to see some of them?"

"Very much so."

"Just a minute." He looked through his pockets. "What did I do with my keys? Probably still in my coat."

He went out, leaving the door open, and turned on the light in the foyer. He was gone for the longest time. In his absence Gregory was tempted to look at the volume on psychometrics again, but he decided not to take the risk. All of a sudden, he heard a scuffling noise—it sounded like something ripping, a piece of material being torn; Sciss appeared in the doorway. He was completely transformed. Straightened up, taking unnaturally long steps, he rushed toward Gregory as if he wanted to attack him. He was breathing noisily. Two steps before he reached Gregory he opened his hand. Something white fell out of it—a crumpled scrap of paper. Gregory recognized the napkin. Floating gently downward, it fell onto the floor. The corners of Sciss's narrow lips were contracted in an expression of unspeakable loathing. Gregory's cheeks and face began to burn as if they had been scalded.

"What do you want from me, you worm?" Sciss screamed in a falsetto voice, almost choking on the words. "A confession? Here's your confession: it was me. Do you hear? It was me! All me! I planned it, set it up, and got rid of the bodies. I played with the corpses as if they were dolls—I felt like doing it, do you understand? Only don't come near me, you worm, because I might vomit!!!" His face was livid. Backing up to the desk and supporting himself on it, he fell into a chair; with trembling hands he plucked a glass vial out of his watch pocket, pulled the cork out with his teeth, panting, and sucked in a few drops of the oily liquid. His breathing slowly eased and became deeper. Propping his head against a row of books on the shelf and spreading his legs apart, he forced himself to breathe more regularly. His eyes were closed. Finally he came to himself and sat up. Gregory's face was burning; he watched without moving from his place.

"Go away. Please go away," Sciss said in a hoarse voice, not opening his eyes. Gregory couldn't move—it was as if he had taken root in the floor. He stood silently, waiting for God knows what.

"You won't go? All right then!" Sciss stood up, coughing and gasping violently. He stretched himself, touched his shirt collar, which he had unbuttoned just a moment before, smoothed out his suit, and walked into the foyer. A moment later the outside door slammed.

Gregory was alone in the apartment, free to look through the drawers, the whole desk; he walked over to it, but even as he did so he knew he wasn't going to search it. Lighting a cigarette he paced from wall to wall, trying unsuccessfully to think. He crushed the cigarette, looked around, shook his head, and went into the foyer. His coat was lying on the floor; when he picked it up he saw that it had been torn almost in half by a strong pull along the back; the loop and a small fragment of material were still on the hanger. He was standing with the coat in his hand when the telephone began to ring. He listened intently. The telephone kept ringing. He went back into the room and waited for it to stop, but the ringing continued. "Too few scruples and not enough results," he thought. "I'm a snake. No, what was it? A worm." He picked up the receiver.

"Hello."

"You? How is it that . . ." He recognized Sheppard's voice.

"Yes, it's me. How . . . how did you know I was here?" Gregory asked. He suddenly became aware that his knees felt like rubber.

"Where else would you be in the middle of the night if you weren't at home," Sheppard answered. "Will you be there long? Is Sciss around?"

"No, Sciss isn't here. He's not in the apartment at all."

"Well, who is? His sister?" Sheppard's tone was severe.

"No, no one at all . . ."

"What did you say? You're there alone? How did you get in?" Suspicion and distaste were evident in the Chief Inspector's voice.

"We came here together, but he . . . walked out. We had . . . there was an argument," Gregory said with great difficulty. "I . . . then, that is, tomorrow, I'll be able . . . oh, the hell with it. What's wrong? Why did you call?"

"Well, it happened. Williams is dead. You know who I mean."

"I know."

"He regained consciousness before he died and wanted to make a statement. I tried everything to get hold of you—I even sent out a radio call."

"I . . . I'm sorry, I didn't know . . ."

"There's nothing to apologize for. We taped the statement. I want you to hear it."

"Today?"

"Why not? Are you waiting for Sciss?"

"No, no . . . I was just going to leave. . . ."

"Good. If you feel up to it, I want you to come over to my house right now. I'd rather not put this off until tomorrow."

"I'll be right over," said Gregory in a dull voice. Then, remembering his coat, he added quickly:

"I have to stop at my place first. It'll only take half an hour."

Sheppard hung up. Gregory returned to the foyer, picked up his coat, threw it over his arm, and ran down the stairs. A quick look into the courtyard showed that the gray Chrysler was gone. He caught a taxi around the corner and went to the Savoy, where he transferred to the Buick. The motor was cold; listening intently to its rumbling while trying to get it started, he could only think about one thing: what would Sheppard say.

There was a no-parking sign on the street outside the Fenshawe house, but he ignored it, running up to the front door along a wet sidewalk that glistened like a mirror in the reflected light of the street lamps. He tried unsuccessfully to unlock the front door with his key, realizing with surprise that it was open. That had never happened before. The big entrance hall, usually completely dark, was faintly lit by a slow-moving, flickering reflection that rhythmically dimmed and intensified on the vaulted ceiling high above the stairs. Walking on tiptoe, Gregory went upstairs, coming to a stop at the door to the mirrored drawing room.

Where there had been a table before, now there was a platform covered with rugs, a row of lit candles along each side of it. In the corner mirrors, the reflected glow of the candles was heightened by the glimmering of the street lights outside. The air was filled with the odor of melted tallow; blue and yellow flames fluttered restlessly. The whole sight was so unexpected that Gregory stood immobilized for a long while, staring at the empty, oblong space between the double row of candles. He looked up slowly, seemingly counting the rainbow-colored sparks flaring up and waning in the low-hanging chandelier, then looked around—the room was deserted. He had to pass through it; sneaking along the wall, he moved on tiptoe like a burglar, his foot brushing against an indistinct, coiled, thin, twisted, whitish-colored wood shaving. Just as he reached the open door he heard the sound of footsteps approaching. Quickening his pace in the hope of reaching his room without a meeting, he saw some yellow sparks flickering in the dimness in front of him; an instant later Mrs. Fenshawe appeared in the room. She was walking slowly, a purple shawl embroidered with shimmering gold sequins flung over her black dress. Gregory didn't know what to do; he wanted to avoid her but there was no way to get past. She seemed to be in a trance; he backed up to get out of her way and kept walking backward, with Mrs. Fenshawe striding along beside him, apparently unaware of his presence. Stumbling against the edge of a rug, Gregory came to a stop. They were back among the mirrors.

"My life!" Mrs. Fenshawe burst into tears. "My life! Too soon! Too soon! They took him away!" She drew so close to him that he could feel her breath on his face. "He knew he couldn't hold out much longer; he knew, he knew, and even today he told me so! Today started like every other day, why couldn't it have gone on that way? Why?!" She repeated this over and over, burning his face with her breath, until finally the words, though they were uttered from deep pain, stopped having any meaning for him.

"Oh . . . I didn't know . . . I'm very sorry," Gregory mumbled, completely at a loss, feeling that he had gotten stuck in an absurdity of some kind, an incomprehensible misfortune, a theater of unreal events and real despair. Mrs. Fenshawe stretched out her dark, tendinous hand from under the shawl and grabbed him violently by the wrist.

"What happened? Did Mr. . . . Mr. . . ." He didn't finish—her voiceless sobbing and the spasmodic movements of her head were answer enough. "It was so sudden," he mumbled. The word brought her around. She stared at him with a strained, insistent, almost hate-filled look.

"No! Not sudden! Not sudden! No! Years, sir, years, and he always managed to avert it, we postponed it together; he had the best care a human being could have. I massaged him every night, and when it was very bad I held his hand until dawn, I sat with him. He wasn't able to stay by himself except in the daytime; he didn't need me during the day, but now of course it's nighttime, it's night!!!" She began screaming horribly again, her voice prolonged in an unnatural ringing echo. "Night . . ." The cry was audibly interrupted and distorted somewhere in the depths of the house, somewhere in the darkness of the rooms that opened on the staircase, somewhere above the head of the woman, who was digging into Gregory's wrist convulsively and pounding his chest with her other hand. Astounded, choked by such frankness, such outspokenness, and such deep despair, Gregory was beginning to understand everything. He stared at the moving flames that lit up the empty, rug-covered place in the middle of the room.

"Help me, oh please help me!" Mrs. Fenshawe called out, whether to God or to him Gregory didn't know, and suddenly her cries were drowned in sobs. One of her tears, shining in the candlelight, fell on the lapel of his suit. Her weeping brought relief for both of them. In a moment Mrs. Fenshawe calmed down, and in an amazingly peaceful although shaky voice, she said:

"Thank you. I'm very sorry. Please . . . please go. No one will bother you. No one! Oh . . . there's no one . . ."

With these words her voice came dangerously close to the crazy screaming again. Gregory was terrified, but Mrs. Fenshawe, gathering up the folds of her purple shawl, went toward the opposite door. He reached the hallway and, almost breaking into a run, rushed to his room, closing the door carefully and firmly behind him.

Safe inside, Gregory turned on the small lamp and sat at his desk, staring at it until his eyes were dazzled by the light.

So he was sick and had died. Some kind of prolonged, peculiar, chronic illness. She'd been nursing him. Only at night—in the daytime he wanted to be by himself. What was wrong with him? Maybe asthma or some other kind of breathing disorder. She mentioned massages. Something to do with the nerves? Insomnia too, or maybe he had heart trouble. He looked so healthy though—that is, he didn't seem to be sick. How old could he have been? Around seventy, at least. It must have happened today—that is, yesterday. Gregory hadn't been home for almost twenty-four hours; the death must have occurred that morning or afternoon, and the body had been taken away in the evening. Otherwise, why the candles?

Gregory's legs were beginning to fall asleep. "It's all clear now," he thought. "He was sick and she was nursing him, some kind of complicated, all-night treatment, but when did she sleep?"

Suddenly remembering that Sheppard was still waiting, he sprang to his feet. He grabbed an old coat from his closet, threw it on, and walked out on tiptoe. The house was still. The candles in the drawing room were beginning to burn out; he made his way downstairs in the remnants of their light. When he got into the car he was amazed to discover that the whole commotion had lasted less than a half hour. He passed Westminster at one o'clock.

Sheppard himself opened the door, same as last time. They walked upstairs in silence.

"I'm sorry you had to wait so long," Gregory said while hanging up his coat, "but my landlord died and I had to . . . uh . . . pay my respects."

Sheppard nodded his head coldly and pointed toward an open door. The room hadn't changed—but with the lights on the collection of photographs looked different, and it occurred to Gregory that there was something pretentious about them. Still not saying anything, Sheppard sat down behind his desk; it was covered with papers and folders. For the moment Gregory remained under the spell of the dark, funereal atmosphere of the Fenshawe house, the unexpectedly silent wall opposite his bed, and the dying candles. He rubbed his wrist involuntarily, as if trying to wipe away the remaining traces of Mrs. Fenshawe's touch. Sitting down opposite the Chief Inspector, he realized for the first time that night how tired he was. All at once it occurred to him that Sheppard was waiting for an account of his visit with Sciss. He responded to the thought as reluctantly as he would have to a demand that he betray someone very dear to him.

"I spent the evening tailing Sciss," he began slowly, then

stopped abruptly and studied the Chief Inspector's face. "Should I go on?" he asked.

"I think it would be useful."

Gregory nodded his head. It was hard for him to describe the evening's events, so he dispensed with commentary and kept to the details. Sheppard leaned back in his chair and listened; only once, when he heard about the photograph, was there any sign of a reaction.

Gregory paused, but the Chief Inspector remained silent. When he finished, he looked up and saw a smile disappearing from Sheppard's face.

"Well, did you finally get him to confess?" the Chief Inspector asked. "As far as I can tell, you stopped suspecting Sciss at the very moment that he left you alone in his apartment. I'm right, aren't I?"

Gregory was stunned. He wrinkled his brow, not certain how to reply. The Chief Inspector was right, but until now he himself hadn't been aware of the change in his thinking about Sciss.

"Yes," he muttered. "I guess so. Anyway, even before then I didn't have much hope of accomplishing anything. I was following the path of least resistance, that's all. I latched on to poor Sciss because there was no one else and I needed a suspect; who knows?—maybe I deliberately tried to compromise him. It's possible—I don't know why, maybe to get the upper hand in my own mind." Gregory became more and more confused. "I know that none of this makes any sense," he finished. "In the long run I don't know a thing about Sciss, not even what he's capable of doing."

"Would you like to know?" the Chief Inspector asked in a sarcastic voice. "You might find him visiting his mother's grave, or trying to pick up a prostitute near Picadilly. That's more or less his range. I don't want to sound like your po-

199

lice auntie, but in this line of work you really should be prepared for an occasional moral hangover. Now, what do you want to do next?"

Gregory shrugged his shoulders.

"A few weeks ago I was pushing all of you, warning about trouble from the press and the public," Sheppard continued, playing with a small metal ruler. "But this time none of what I expected came to pass, in fact nothing came of it at all. There were a couple of articles connecting the case to flying saucers and—paradoxically—that was the end of the publicity. A few letters to the editor—and it was over. I hadn't realized how indifferent we've become to the extraordinary nowadays. If a moon walk is possible, so is everything else. So we're on our own with this case, Lieutenant, and we might as well just shelve it quietly. . . ."

"Is that what you called to tell me?"

The Chief Inspector didn't say anything.

After a moment or so Gregory answered his own question.

"You wanted me to hear what Williams said, right? Maybe . . . I should go now. It's very late and I don't want to take up any more of your time."

Sheppard rose to his feet, opened a flat case containing a tape recorder, and connected the speaker.

"The recording was made at his request," he said to Gregory. "The technicians were in a rush and the recorder wasn't working too well, so the sound isn't the best. You'd better move closer. Now listen to this."

He threaded the tape into the spool, plugged in the extension cord, and adjusted the modulation knob; the recorder pulsated a few times; a steady hum emanated from the speaker, followed by several knocks and some scratching noises, and at last a far-off voice, distorted as if it was coming through a metal tube.

"May I speak now? Commissioner, Doctor, may I? I had

200

a good flashlight . . . my wife gave it to me just this year, for the night shift. First time I went around he's lying there the usual way, with his hands like this; next time around I hear a crash like a bag of potatoes is falling. I shine my light through the second window—he's on the floor. I figure he must have fell out of the coffin but he's moving already. I think I must be dreaming all this so I rub my eyes with snow, but he keeps shuffling along, falling all over the place as he goes. Commissioner, I don't know how long this went on, but it was long enough, believe me. I kept shining my light but I didn't know if I should go in or not, and there he is, flapping around and turning over and finally he reaches the window and I couldn't see him too good because he was crawling right under the window, making a hell of a racket all the time. Then the shutters come open."

An indistinct voice in the background asked something; it was difficult to make out the words.

"That I don't know," resounded a voice closer to the microphone. "And I didn't see if any glass was falling either. Maybe it did, but I can't say. I was standing over on the side, I can't . . . can't manage to show you. So I was standing this way and he was sitting or whatever he was doing this way—all I could see was his head—I could have touched it, Commissioner, it was closer to me than this here table is. I shined my light inside and lit the place up real good and there was nothing there, only the empty coffin with some shavings in it and nothing else and no one was there. I lean over and take a look in the window and there he is down below me; his legs going a dozen ways at the same time and he's rocking back and forth like a drunk, Doctor, he's crawling along on his side and tapping away, like a blind man tapping his cane, except he was doing it with his hands. Or maybe he had something. 'Halt,' I says to him, 'what d'you think you're doing, what's going on here?' —that's what I said, or something like that."

A short silence followed, except for a steady, delicate creaking, as if someone was scratching the microphone with a needle.

"He climbs up a bit, then falls over again. Like I told you, I ordered him to stop, but he wasn't alive; at first I thought maybe he wasn't dead and had just now woke up in the coffin, but he wasn't alive, he didn't have any eyes like, I mean only—you know what I mean, so he couldn't see anything and he didn't feel anything. I mean if he could feel he wouldn't keep banging himself around on those boards, and he was banging away like the devil himself was inside him. I yelled something at him—I don't even know what— and he kept turning this way and that way and finally he grabs the windowsill with his teeth— What?"

Once again a muffled, indistinct voice asking questions; only the last word was comprehensible: ". . . teeth?"

"So I shined my light on his face from close up, it was kind of blurred like, well, kind of like a dead fish, and what happened next I don't know."

Another voice, closer and lower, asked:

"When did you draw your pistol? Did you try to shoot him?"

"My pistol? I can't say if I drew it or not because I don't remember. You say I ran away? How did that happen? I don't know. What's this on my eye? Doc . . . doctor . . ."

A far-off voice.

". . . there's nothing there, Williams. Close your eyes, that's good; you'll feel better in a minute."

A woman's voice from the back:

"He's done for, he's done for."

Again Williams's voice, breathing faster:

"I can't go on like this. If it . . . am I done for? Is my wife here? No? Why not? She is? What damned good are the regulations if they don't say nothing about . . . this . . . they don't cover . . ."

The sounds of a brief dispute could be heard; someone said out loud:

"That's enough!" Another voice interrupted:

"Did you see the car, Williams, the headlights?"

"Car . . . what car?" Williams repeated in a weak, stuttering voice. "I can't get it out of my head, how he was rocking back and forth on his side and couldn't do nothing, and how he was dragging those shavings along with him . . . if there was a rope I might have understood it, but there wasn't no rope . . ."

"What rope?"

"A doormat? No. Rope? I don't know. Where? God, no one ever saw anything like it. He looked like he didn't like the light shining on him, but that's impossible, Commissioner, isn't it? The shavings—no! Straw . . . won't . . . hold . . ."

A long silence, interrupted by scratching, blurred noises —it sounded as if several persons were carrying on a furious whispered conversation at some distance from the microphone. A short choking, the sound of hiccups, and suddenly the voice was gruffer:

"I'll give it all away, I don't want anything for myself. Where is she? Is this her hand? Is that you?"

Again scratching, tapping as if something heavy was being moved, the sound of cracking glass, the hiss of escaping gas, some sharp static, then a deafening bass voice uttering the words:

"Turn it off, there won't be any more."

Sheppard stopped the reels, the tape stood still. He returned to his place behind the desk. Gregory was hunched over, pressing his hand against the arm of the chair and staring at his own whitened knuckles. He seemed to have forgotten about Sheppard.

"If I could only turn everything back," he thought. "The whole thing, all of it, to about a month ago—no, not enough, maybe a year. Ridiculous. I can't escape. . . ."

"Chief Inspector," he said at last, "if you had picked someone else instead of me, you'd probably have a perpetrator locked up for this by now. Do you understand what I'm talking about?"

"Maybe. Why don't you continue."

"Continue? When I was studying physics, the section on optical illusions in my textbook had an illustration that was either a white wine glass against a dark background or two dark human profiles against a white background. You only saw one or the other, and as a student I took it for granted that only one of the two images was genuine, although to this day I still can't say which. That's funny, isn't it, Chief Inspector? Do you remember the conversation about order we once had in this room? About the natural order of things. You said that the natural order can be imitated."

"No, you said that."

"Did I? Maybe so. But what if it isn't really that way? What if there isn't anything to imitate? What if the world isn't scattered around us like a jigsaw puzzle—what if it's like a soup with all kinds of things floating around in it, and from time to time some of them get stuck together by chance to make some kind of whole? What if everything that exists is fragmentary, incomplete, aborted, events with ends but no beginnings, events that only have middles, things that have fronts or rears but not both, with us constantly making categories, seeking out, and reconstructing, until we think we can see total love, total betrayal and defeat, although in reality we are all no more than haphazard fractions. Our faces and our fates are shaped by statistics— we human beings are the resultant of Brownian motion— incomplete sketches, randomly outlined projections. Perfection, fullness, excellence are all rare exceptions—they occur only because there is such an excess, so unimaginably much of everything! The daily commonplace is automatically regulated by the world's vastness, its infinite variety; because of it, what we see as gaps and breaches complement each other; the mind, for its own self-preservation, finds and integrates scattered fragments. Using religion and philosophy as the cement, we perpetually collect and assemble all the garbage comprised by statistics in order to make sense out of things, to make everything respond in one unified voice like a bell chiming to our glory. But it's only soup. . . . The mathematical order of the universe is our answer to the pyramids of chaos. On every side of us we see bits of life that are completely beyond our understanding—we label them unusual, but we really don't want to acknowledge them. The only thing that really exists is statistics. The intelligent person is the statistical person. Will a child be beautiful or ugly? Will he enjoy music? Will he get cancer? It's all decided by a throw of the dice. At the very moment of our conception—statistics! Statistics determine which clusters of genes our bodies will be created from, statistics determine when we're going to die. A normal statistical distribution decides everything: whether I'm going to meet a woman and fall in love, how long I'm going to live, maybe even whether I'm going to be immortal. From time to time, it may be, statistics participate in some things blindly, by accident—beauty and lameness, for example. But explicit processes will cease to exist before long: soon even despair, beauty, happiness, and ugliness will result from statistics. Our knowledge is underlined by statistics—nothing exists except blind chance, the eternal arrangement of fortuitous patterns. An infinite number of Things taunt our fondness for Order. Seek, and ye shall find; in the end ye shall always find, if you only look with enough fervor; statistics doesn't exclude anything, and therefore it renders everything possible, or more or less probable. History, on the other hand, comes true by Brownian motion, a statistical dance of particles that never stop dreaming about another temporal world. . . ."

"Maybe even God only exists from time to time," the Chief Inspector added quietly. He had leaned forward, and with his face averted was listening attentively to what Gregory was spewing forth with such difficulty from deep inside himself.

"Maybe," Gregory replied indifferently. "But the gaps in his existence are very wide, you know."

He stood up, walked over to the wall, and stared at a photograph without seeing it.

"Maybe even we . . ." he began hesitantly, "even we only exist from time to time; I mean: sometimes less, sometimes almost disappearing, dissolving, and then, with a sudden spasm, a sudden spurt that disintegrates the memory center, we merge for a moment . . . for a day . . . and we become—"

He stopped abruptly. After a moment he spoke again in a different tone of voice.

"Forgive me for going on like that. It's all nonsense. Maybe . . . I've had it for today. I think it's time for me to go."

"Can't you stay a little longer?"

Gregory paused. He gave Sheppard a surprised look.

"I suppose so, but it's been a long day; I think—"

"Do you know Mailer trucking?"

"Mailer?"

"Big trucks with red and gold stripes. You must have seen them."

"Oh sure, 'Mailer Goes Anywhere.' " Gregory recalled the slogan in their ads. "What about it?" He didn't finish.

Not moving from his chair, Sheppard handed him a newspaper and pointed to a short paragraph at the bottom of the page. "Yesterday afternoon a Mailer Company truck crashed into a freight train near Amber. The driver, who drove onto the railroad tracks even though he had seen the warning signal, was killed instantly. None of the train crew was hurt."

Gregory looked up at the Chief Inspector with a puzzled expression.

"He was probably on his way back to Tunbridge Wells with an empty truck. Mailer has a garage there," said Sheppard. "About a hundred vehicles. They transport food in refrigerator trucks, mostly meat and fish. The deliveries are made at night so the shipment will be available in the morning. Each truck has a driver and a helper—they usually start out sometime in the late evening."

"The paper only mentions a driver," Gregory said slowly. He still didn't understand any of this.

"That's right. After the truck is unloaded, the driver takes it back to the garage, and the helper stays behind to help move the cargo into the warehouse."

"The helper was lucky," Gregory said indifferently.

"That's for sure. These people work very hard. They have to keep their trucks rolling in all kinds of weather. Mailer services four routes—they form a cross on the map: Bromley and Lovering to the north, Dover to the east, Horsham and Lewes in the west, and Brighton in the south."

"What's the point of all this?" Gregory asked.

"Each driver has a regular schedule. He's on every third and fifth night, and he gets compensatory time off if road conditions are bad. The drivers weren't too lucky this winter. Maybe you remember, there wasn't any snow at all at the beginning of January. We had a little snow around the third week of January, and we got quite a bit of it in February. The more trouble the highway department has clearing the snow off the roads, the longer it takes the trucks to cover their routes. Their average speed was about fifty miles per hour at the beginning of January, it fell to thirty-five in

February; and in March, when the thaw set in and the roads were covered with ice, it dropped another ten miles per hour."

"What are you getting at?" Gregory asked uncomfortably. He was leaning against the desk with his hands spread wide apart, staring at the Chief Inspector. Sheppard gave him a bland look and asked:

"Did you ever drive a car in a thick fog?"

"Of course. What—"

"In that case you know what hard work it is. For hours on end there's nothing but pea soup in front of your windshield. No matter how hard you try, you can't see a thing. Some people open their doors and drive while leaning out, but it doesn't do any good. You have to depend on intuition to tell you where the sides of the road are; the fog diffuses the light of your headlights and in the end you can hardly tell whether you're going forward, sideways, or uphill; the fog is constantly rolling and swirling around you and your eyes start tearing from the strain of trying to see through it. After a while you start seeing things—strange things . . . moving shadows, weird shapes deep in the fog; all alone in a dark car you lose your perception, you can hardly feel your own body—you can't even tell if your hands are still on the steering wheel and you begin to feel numb—fear is the only thing that keeps you going. So you keep driving that way, with the sweat dripping down your back and face, the motor droning monotonously in your ears, alternately dozing off and waking up with a spasmodic twitch. It's like a nightmare. Try to imagine what it's like to go through that year after year. Furthermore, imagine that a long time ago you began seeing things, having visions, peculiar thoughts that you wouldn't dare tell anyone about, confide in anyone . . . thoughts about the world maybe, or about things no one should believe in, or about how you should have acted toward other people while they were still alive or even now that they're dead. During the day, at work, when you're fully conscious, you realize that these are nothing but hallucinations, fantasies, and like any normal person you suppress them. But the thoughts go on living inside you, they appear in your dreams, they become more and more persistent. You learn how to hide them, you're afraid that your reputation will be ruined if anyone finds out about them. You don't want to be different from anyone else. Then you get a chance to earn a good salary by working nights, but of course you have to remain awake and alert all night; when you're driving through the moors, you have plenty of time to think, especially when you're alone in an empty eight-ton truck and can't distract yourself by making small talk with the helper when you really . . . So there you are driving your truck month after month; autumn passes, winter comes, and you're caught in a thick fog for the first time. You try to shake yourself free of the hallucinations, you stop the truck, get out, rub your face and forehead with snow, and drive on. Hours go by. The fog is like milk all around you; it's as if you're surrounded by an overflowing, infinite whiteness—as if such things as ordinary roads, muddy, lit-up streets, small towns, houses never existed. You're all alone, completely and eternally alone in the dark little cab of your truck and you stare frontward, blinking your eyes, trying to rub something out of them that becomes clearer and clearer, more and more insistent no matter how much you try. You're driving and driving, and the vision goes on for an hour, maybe two, maybe three; finally there comes a moment in which it is so compelling, so uncontrollable, that it seizes you, it becomes you, and soon you feel better, you finally know what has to be done, so you stop the truck and get out . . ."

"What the hell are you talking about?" Gregory shouted. He was trembling.

"There are 218 drivers working out of the Mailer garage

in Tunbridge Wells. In a group that big there'll always be at least one who . . . who's a little different. Who—let's say —is not completely healthy. What do you think about it?"

Sheppard was calm; he was speaking in an even, almost monotonous tone, but there was something relentless in his voice.

"The incidents all took place between midnight and dawn in small provincial mortuaries. Aside from a few differences in detail, the individual cases are tied together by one connecting link—a certain consistency that no human being could have planned. No one, no human mind would have been capable of doing any of this. We've already agreed about that, haven't we?

"Now, let's look at the case in the light of certain unusual circumstances surrounding it. First, a driver's work schedule. Second, each consecutive incident took place farther and farther away from the 'center,' Tunbridge Wells, and almost at the center of the 'center' we find the Mailer garage, with empty trucks pulling in regularly from midnight on. Why did each subsequent incident take place farther and farther away from the 'center'? Because the average speed of the trucks was decreasing, and even though they always left Tunbridge Wells at about the same time, the drivers were getting to their destinations later and later and as a result were beginning their return trips later and later; consequently, it was taking them longer to cover the same distance."

"How do you know?" Gregory interrupted.

"From the fact that the fog is at its worst for a period of about two hours every night. This is the period in which it is most effective in inducing fantasies and delusions in drivers making their return trips alone. Even so, if road conditions are good on the return trip, the two-hour period doesn't affect them as much as it does when the roads are covered with snow. So we find another regular item: the more resistance the snow offers to the tires of the truck, the less resistance the driver offers to the two-hour fantasy-producing period. Furthermore, the more snow on the road, the lower the temperature, and the lower the temperature, the worse the truck's motor performs; therefore, we find, we get a constant if we multiply the difference in temperature by the product of the time between two incidents and the distance from the center to the site of an incident. As road conditions deteriorate, the dispatcher at the Mailer garage gives the drivers longer breaks between trips. Even so, on each subsequent trip the driver has less and less endurance during the two-hour period, and as a result he covers less and less distance. The second coefficient—the time between two trips counted in days—increases proportionately, and that's why the product remains the same, speaking roughly."

"In other words . . . one of the drivers . . . is a paranoiac, is that it? He works on the night shift, stops his truck somewhere along the way and steals a body . . . but what did he do with them?"

"At dawn, when he drove out of the foggy area, he regained his senses—he was coming back into the ordinary world—so he did his best to dump the evidence of his night of insanity. There were plenty of opportunities—after all, he was covering quite a bit of territory, with plenty of hills, shallow ravines, thickets, rivers, bushes. . . . Terrified, unable to believe what had happened, he would resolve to get help for himself, but he was afraid he'd lose his job, so when the dispatcher gave him the date of his next trip he wouldn't say a word and right on schedule he'd be back behind the wheel again. He must have known the topography of the whole region by memory—every road, every estate, every grade crossing, every building—he knew exactly where all the cemeteries were located. . . ."

Gregory's gaze moved from the Chief Inspector's face to the open newspaper.

"That's him," he said.

"The madness must have increased steadily," Sheppard answered slowly. "The memory of deeds committed, anxiety that he would be exposed, growing distrust of his friends and co-workers, sick interpretations of innocent things other people said to him—everything must have combined to make his condition worse, to increase the tension in which he was living. You can see that it must have been getting harder and harder for him to come back to his senses; his condition was deteriorating steadily, his attention span was decreasing, he was less able to concentrate and more likely to become a victim of circumstances. For example—this guy—"

Gregory suddenly walked away from the desk and sat down on a chair near the bookshelf, drawing his hand over his face.

"So that's how it happened," he said. "An imitation of a miracle . . . ha, ha . . . is all this true?"

"No," Sheppard replied serenely, "but it might be. Or, strictly speaking, it can become the truth."

"What are you trying to say? Come on, Chief Inspector, I've had enough fooling around."

"This isn't my theory, Gregory. Calm down. Out of six incidents—are you paying attention?—out of six incidents, this truck driver,"—he tapped the newspaper—"was definitely on the road near the place in question three times. In other words, three of the times, during the hours just before dawn, he drove past the places where the corpses disappeared."

"What about the other times?" Gregory asked. Something strange was happening inside him. An unexpected feeling of relief, of hope, was expanding his chest; it seemed to him that he was breathing more easily.

"The other times? Well . . . about one incident . . .

Lewes . . . we don't know anything. For the second, the dead truck driver had . . . an alibi."

"An alibi?"

"Yes. Not only did he have the night off but he was in Scotland for three days. We checked—there's no doubt about it."

"Then it wasn't him!" Gregory stood up, he had to get on his feet; the jolt resulting from this movement knocked the newspaper off the edge of the desk.

"No, it wasn't him. To be sure it wasn't him, unless we classify that incident separately."

The Chief Inspector took a quick look at Gregory, whose face was contorted in anger. "But if we don't do that, if it wasn't Mailer—the Mailer driver—there are still plenty of other vehicles circulating in the region at night: post office trucks, ambulances, emergency vehicles, buses . . . we have an endless quantity of phenomena that can be fitted into the theory."

"Are you making fun of me?" Gregory asked.

"Of course not, I'm trying to help you," answered the Chief Inspector.

"Thank you."

Gregory bent down and picked up the paper.

"So this truck driver was, that is, allegedly was," he corrected himself, "a paranoiac; in other words, sick according to all normal standards: fog times frost times insanity . . ." He glanced at Sheppard with a strange smile.

"And what if, by chance, purely by chance, he took a different route the other times—I mean a route that didn't go anywhere near the mortuaries—would he still be a suspect . . . still a sacrificial lamb . . ."

Gregory sneered; he was walking around the room.

"I must know," he said. "I have to know . . . right now!"

He grabbed the newspaper again and flattened it out.

"The first page is missing," Sheppard noted, "but I can give you the details. It's yesterday's paper."

"Oh!"

"No, I didn't invent any of this. Everything I told you was verified yesterday. We worked on it all day, both the local police, and Farquart, who flew up to Scotland to check out the driver's alibi, if you're interested."

"No, no, but . . . I want to know why you did all this."

"Well, in the final analysis . . . well, because I work at Scotland Yard also," said Sheppard.

Gregory appeared not to have heard the answer; in a state of obvious agitation he walked around the room, stopping to stare at the photograph.

"You don't understand what I mean. . . . This is really convenient, very, very convenient . . . exactly what we needed. There is a perpetrator after all, but he's dead so we can't question him or continue the investigation . . . a very humane solution—no miscarriage of justice possible, no one suffers. . . . Did you really suspect him? Did you also . . . or did you only want something to match the facts that we were stuck with, the facts that forced us to take action in the first place, so you could give a semblance of order to this disorder and mark an open case closed with a nice sense of orderliness. Is that what it's all about?"

"I don't see any alternative," said Sheppard indifferently. He seemed to have had enough of the conversation and was no longer looking at Gregory, who had stopped walking, occupied with a new thought.

"Of course it's possible to interpret it your way too," he said. "Of course! You know, I believe it when you say you want to help me. At first we couldn't do anything with this case—not a thing—and now we can. Maybe we can shake that alibi. Or if we eliminate that one exceptional incident

214

from the series, and maybe the other exceptions with it, the investigation moves out of the dead end. The odds are it's an illness! You can use illness to explain the most peculiar things, even visions and stigmata, even . . . even miracles! You know the works of Guggenheimer, Hopley, and Wintershield, don't you? They're not in our library, but you must have read them."

"The psychiatrists? Which of their books did you have in mind—they wrote quite a few."

"The ones in which they analyze the Gospels to prove that Jesus was crazy. They created quite a stir in their time. A psychiatric analysis of Scripture leading to a diagnosis of paranoia . . ."

"Let me give you some advice," said Sheppard. "These biblical analogies won't get you anywhere. Maybe you could afford that kind of thing at the beginning of the case when you wanted to make the problem more interesting, but the investigation is over now, except for a few technicalities. . . ."

"Do you really mean that?" Gregory asked quietly.

"Yes. Because I hope, I feel sure, that you don't want to be left crying in the wilderness. . . ."

"Then what am I supposed to do?" Gregory asked in a slightly deferential tone of voice, straightening up and watching the old man, who was rising from his armchair.

"We have to set up clearly defined guidelines for the future. For the foreseeable future. I'll be waiting for you tomorrow morning at the Yard."

"Like the last time, around ten o'clock?" There was a note of hidden amusement in Gregory's voice.

"Yes. Will you be there?" he added casually. They looked at each other, both standing up. Gregory's lips quivered, but he didn't say anything. He backed up toward the door, then turned his back to Sheppard and placed his hand on the knob, constantly aware of Sheppard's calm and steadfast gaze.

Finally opening the door, he turned and tossed the words over his shoulder.

"I'll be there."